MILENA AGUS is a bestselling ~~...~~ 1959, she now lives in Cagli ~~...~~ Italian and history at a secon ~~...~~ novels, Agus is the recipient of several literary awards, namely the prestigious Zerilli-Marimò prize in New York. Her work has been translated into over twenty languages.

From the Land of the Moon

'Agus sketches her characters lightly, creating an impression-istic and mysterious narrative that probes the tension between imagination and madness and celebrates minor moments of beauty in an absurd and unfair world' *New Yorker*

'Slim but powerful, it conjures up the spirit of Roberto Rossellini' *Time*

'Takes on the feel of Marguerite Duras' powerful little book, *The Lover* – pure passion in an enclosed (emotional and physical) space' *Los Angeles Times*

The House in Via Manno

'Beautiful … For such a little book, the novel covers an extraordinary range of subjects with great depth of understanding' *Sydney Morning Herald*

'Fans of Isabel Allende and Gabriel Garcia Márquez will enjoy this heartwarming story of the loyalties and loves of a large Sardinian family set during World War II' *Vogue*

Milena Agus

While the Shark is Sleeping

Translated from Italian by Brigid Maher

TELEGRAM

Published 2014 by Telegram

1

Copyright © Milena Agus, 2005 and 2014
Translation copyright © Brigid Maher 2014

Published 2006 in Italian as *Mentre dorme il pescecane* by Nottetempo

ISBN 978 1 84659 186 0
eISBN 978 1 84659 187 7

Printed and bound by CPI Group (UK) Ltd, Croydon, CR0 4YY

TELEGRAM
26 Westbourne Grove, London W2 5RH
www.telegrambooks.com

To doctors
Clara Corda and Valter Cicone

'So now what?' Pinocchio asked.

'Now, my boy, we're well and truly done for.'

'What do you mean? Give me your hand, Daddy, and be careful you don't slip.'

'Where are you taking me?'

'We have to try again to escape. Come with me and don't be afraid.'

From *The Adventures of Pinocchio* by Carlo Collodi

The Sevilla Mendoza family

Actually we're not the Sevilla Mendoza family at all. We're Sardinian, I'm sure of it, and have been since the Upper Palaeolithic.

My father's the one who calls us that, with the two surnames like they do down there. He's travelled masses and America's the place of his dreams. Not North America, rich and fortunate, but South America, poor and cursed. When he was young he used to say that he'd go back there alone or with the woman he'd marry, who'd share his ideals and the adventure of trying to save the world.

He never asked Mamma to go with him. He's gone wherever they've needed help, but never with her – she's too afraid of the dangers and always lacking in strength.

At our house everyone's pursuing something: for Mamma, it's beauty; for Papà, South America; for my brother, perfection; for Zia – my auntie – a boyfriend.

I write stories because when I don't like this world here, I move into my own and I feel great.

And there are a lot of things I don't like about this world. In fact, I'd go so far as to say that it's ugly and I much prefer my own.

In my world, there's also him. He already has a wife.

I absolutely must not forget what he said.

'Swear to me you don't want to have a romantic relationship with me.'

And me: 'I swear.'

'Ours will be an animal connection, not a vegetable one.'

'An animal connection.'

'Two dogs that wag their tails and smell each other's arses when they meet.'

'Do you think I'm beautiful?' I ask him.

'The most beautiful woman here.'

'But I'm the only one here.'

'So?'

'Please, tell me if you think I'm beautiful.'

'Your arse is the best in the world.'

But my arse is not my idea of love.

'What about my face, do you like my face?'

'With an arse like that why would I give a damn about your face? Besides, if there's one thing that gives me the shits it's giving compliments on command.'

So then I stop, because I don't want to behave like Mamma.

Nonna says Mamma has always been a bit of a pain in the neck. When she was little, before going to bed she would give her parents a kiss and say good night. They might be tired and respond in distracted tones: 'Good night.'

'Give me a proper good night!' the child would beg.

'Good night,' they'd say, a bit irritated.

'Not like that, not like that! That was even worse than before!' And she'd become desperate and cry until my grandparents, exhausted, gave her a good hiding. Only then, when there was nothing else for it, would she fall asleep.

She wakes at dawn and goes out onto the terrace with a bucket of bleach and a broom to clean up the pigeons' 'pooeys'. She's kind even to them. She invites them to leave by building a barrier of spiky red and white plants, perfectly matching the brick paving, all the way around the sides of the terrace. Or she hangs plastic bags from threads, so that the rustling scares them away. And all the other flowers are red and white too: jasmine, roses, tulips, freesias, dahlias.

Colours are important to her even when she's hanging out the washing. But here I don't think it's a question of aesthetics. For washing belonging to us children, for instance, she always uses green pegs, for hope. For her and Papà's sheets, it's red pegs, for passion. I've noticed that she always avoids the yellow ones – despair – and I've realised that when she finds them in the assorted packs, she gets rid of them.

Mamma is not only afraid of yellow pegs but of everything. It's unusual for her to watch a film through to the end without rushing terrified out of the cinema during the first heavy, or even simply realistic, scene.

She's also afraid of the stars, because she understands astrology and she anxiously examines their course and position. It's very rare for the skies not to offer her some cause for concern.

She always says she'll never forgive herself for not giving birth to my brother a few hours later: the skies would have offered a superb aspect between Venus and a moon, both in exaltation, which would have made him happy in love. She feels guilty about me too, because in my case just an hour earlier would have been enough.

'I should have asserted myself,' she always used to say. 'I had labour pains but I didn't want to be a nuisance. They were sure I wasn't ready but it wasn't true. I gave birth to the girl without any pain, at a moment when the moon was squared by all the planets. My poor daughter!'

My father says she's a rabbit and poos in little balls. He often goes up to her and whispers the sound she makes when she's eating carrots – 'Nyum nyum nyum nyum nyum nyum nyum nyum' – and Mamma laughs and laughs and looks at him enraptured, because he's her opposite. He doesn't give a shit about what other people think and he makes no apologies for anything. And he never feels inferior to anyone, not even for not having a degree. In fact, when someone shows off their qualifications he says that's not learning, learning is something else and they're completely ignorant.

'We need to tread carefully around your mother,' Papà confided to me once. 'Anyone who has anything to do with her has to be given an information sheet. Directions for use. If I ever had any problems, if I was ever sad and could no longer manage to make her laugh, I'd really rather be in the worst place on earth rummaging through the garbage.'

That's why we never share any secrets with her and instead act as a filter between her and the world.

I, on the other hand, have an iron stomach. Like my maternal grandfather, Nonno, who fought in the Navy during the war – three shipwrecks, two years in a German prison, the last few months with the SS, no less, marching day and night in icy conditions as they retreated and killed everyone who couldn't make it. He fought with dogs for a bit of potato skin out of the garbage while 'Splinter' looked on in enjoyment. He walked without stopping and that's why they didn't kill him and he made it through.

He came back and started living again. The only thing is he was nervous. You'd drop a fork at dinner and he'd jump a foot in the air.

He stopped telling my mother about the horrors of war almost immediately, because she was having nightmares and dreamt she was with Nonna in a long line of people ready to be interned while he was being tortured.

In reaction to Hitler's wickedness, Mamma became a communist. But then she read about the crimes of Stalin and Mao and how bad life was in Russia and China. She threw herself into the Church, but there, too, there were bad people, or there had been in the past: for example, the inquisitors, and merciless bigoted women. The only thing left was democracy. Perfect. But Papà always says that Western democracies, through their economic dictatorship, are killing the Third World.

He's already married, but those phone calls cast a spell on me.

'It's me, how are you?'

I can no longer remember how I am. I start looking for ways to fit him in, organising really complicated plans to get him to come to my house when my parents aren't home. Especially Mamma, who's always in if she's not at work. I convince her to go on walks for her painting and I leave her further and further away with her palette: on San Michele hill, which overlooks the whole city, but where Mamma grows sad thinking of how poor Violante Carroz plunged to her death there in 1511, or at the Calamosca lighthouse away on the infinite horizon. Then we make a time and I go and collect her on my red Vespa, because there's no way Mamma could ever get her bearings and catch a bus.

The wait is a real ceremony: ten-watt lamp in the bedroom, total silence. I wait for him stretched out on the bed as though we're about to go out. Overcoat, handbag, high heels, hands crossed over my chest. A dead woman ready to be reborn. A plain girl ready to become beautiful.

Since he can't take me out in public on account of his wife, going out happens in our imagination. Clothes are magic, because they don't depend on the real seasons, but on what you have in mind for that day.

The bell. The code. He enters, gives me a glance that to me seems to say 'You're beautiful', walks the two hallways of the house to my room, picks up the girl lying on the bed and takes her with him into another world.

My brother is often sad. When we're sure Mamma can't hear us, he tells me about his school, which is a very rough place. At morning tea time, the tough kids always eat at least two snacks, while the weak ones don't even get one, otherwise they get bashed up. The snacks my mother prepares for my brother get snatched by the tough kids. And the same with his calculator and other equipment. We're always having to buy new things. He says that if it was up to him he wouldn't go back any more, especially not now that a girl he liked has got together with one of the tough kids. He'd play the piano and that's it.

Mamma used to tell to me about her office with the same sadness. She had to work in the archives.

With the black key she'd open the door of the first room. There was a small safe there that contained rows of keys in various colours that opened the cabinets. One, however, although it was the same colour as some of the others, had a small mark on it and gave access to the second room. Here, too, there was a small safe, containing the keys to access the more delicate documents. Each document had its classification on the computer, but her colleague looked after that. Mamma just had to go and open the cabinets, take the documents to staff who asked for them and make sure everything was returned to its place. But she was slow and her colleagues would grumble, she often tripped over chairs, or fell off the ladder when the shelf was high up, and the documents would end up strewn across the floor. She felt guilty and with ever more exasperating meekness would never ask for holiday leave in August or for a small pay rise. What's more, she hid all this from my father, passing off her November holidays as a quirk, a personal preference.

In the mornings, she'd come into the kitchen looking beaten and would only smile when my father greeted her in good spirits – 'Ah! The freshness! The beauty!' – and he'd sigh, pretending to reach orgasm. He teased her because he knew how much a good morning or a good night in the wrong tone could throw her into despair.

Then she and my brother would prepare to go to the gallows. They'd walk part of the way together and I, heading in the opposite direction, would often turn around to look at them: he would have an enormous backpack on his shoulders, because the tough kid in his class never brought a single book to school, and she always looked like the coat-hanger for her own dress, she wanted so little to exist as a person in that moment.

Then one day my father said, 'We don't give a fucking shit about the peanuts they pay, do we? Lady Sevilla Mendoza is poor, but she's a painter! And an artist can't waste time cooped up in an office.'

I have to say we never noticed any economic change after that. Besides, Mamma sells tons of paintings at exhibitions, people like them a lot, and Papà sends the money from the sales to the Third World, because really, what would we do with it?

Sometimes she stands for hours at the window, with her paintbrush in her hand. She says we're always busy doing something else so we miss the sky, the flocks of birds arriving or migrating. Our house looks out over the roofs and little terraces of the Marina neighbourhood. The terraces are all square, like ours, with flowers and grills for roasting fish on a Sunday and blue tanks because there's never enough water and lots of people always doing something: waterproofing, adding on verandas or unapproved extensions, repairing window frames, putting up new TV antennas. When Nonna comes to visit, she looks out and observes everything and says, 'Have you seen what a nice job they've done down there?' and Mamma feels upset because Nonna has never had a word of praise for our house, not even on any of those beautiful days when she's come by at sunset, when beyond the Marina neighbourhood the sea at the port of Cagliari is watercolour violet and the sky is still and silent and the ship that's departing seems lit up for a ball.

Mamma feels sad when she sees the ships depart; even though no one inside is saying farewell to her she finds it a painful separation. 'That's life,' she sighs. 'There's always someone leaving.'

My father advises her not to watch them anymore,

these departing ships – who gives a fuck about violet sunsets and ballroom lights, Mamma should be looking out at the ships coming in. And it's true that she always smiles, looking out the window of a morning, when the ferries come into the port, which on a calm, clear day seems like a lake because of the way it's closed in at the horizon by the blue mountains of Capoterra on the other side of the gulf.

Nonna says that my brother has inherited the worst of Mamma and Papà: that is, her unease and his detachment. Papà could do great things for him except that he's never around. He could talk to him one on one about God, rather than in general when all of us are present. Or about how to shave without cutting yourself, or how to pick up women. Instead, his world consists only of Mozart, Bach and Beethoven, who are great, but a long way away from our world, plus you need a copy of the music.

To pick up women you need some little song like those Papà plays on his guitar wherever he happens to be, with all the women around him drooling and singing along together. When he's at home my brother stays in his room playing and Mamma goes in and out with juice she's squeezed for him and all these healthy snacks that have the right proportions of carbohydrates, proteins and vitamins. He sends her away, 'Ma, what a drag!'

Nonna says that Mamma married a strange fellow who was off being a volunteer and saving other people's children while his own were being born. He didn't care about that pregnant, terrified girl who would ask the doctors if they thought giving birth was more or less painful than being tortured by the Gestapo, or the KGB, or the CIA. The doctors would reply, 'It depends what kind of torture, signora, it depends. But you have to remember that since the beginning of time, women have been giving birth. That means it's possible.'

Strangeness breeds strangeness. There's no escape. And another thing Nonna can't stand about my brother is the way his clothes are always hanging off him, same with Mamma. They're both so beautiful, but you can't tell because they're clumsy and awkward and they walk so bent over that they don't even look tall.

Nonno was tough. At sixteen, the age my brother is now, he had to leave the village for the Continent to do military service. He'd been boasting about it to the other boys. The day before he left a few of them lay in wait for him and beat him up. So many of them against just one. He left all the same and the adventure of war came along and found him there ready, very early.

What we have in common, Mamma and I, is that we cover everything with honey, whereas Zia is brusque and if she wants to say someone sent someone else away she'll say that 'he gave him a kick up the arse'. We don't like Zia's manner. We like to see the world through a layer of honey and Papà says we'll get diabetes of the brain. I think Mamma and Zia are so different because of what happened at the beginning. When Nonna was pregnant with Mamma, she and Nonno lived with another couple in order to save money on rent. The other lady couldn't have children and had taken a dislike to Nonna. She'd pour boiling water on her flowers, she'd pinch the plates from her good dinner set, so it became more and more diminished over time. This business went on for years until Mamma went to primary school, but you couldn't say anything to Nonno because one time when Nonna had just hinted at the matter, Nonno had gone to confront the neighbour's husband and was ready to kill him. There was nothing for it but to keep quiet and buy more plates, or grow more flowers, when you could. The last thing they lost was the book *The Thousand and One Nights*, which Nonna always put back in a secret place after reading a bit with her little girl. One day it was nowhere to be found.

Whereas when Zia was born, the neighbour had finally fallen pregnant; flowers didn't wither, plates didn't disappear and neither did storybooks. Plus Nonno was less nervous, the concentration camp was further in the past and at dinner Zia could drop all the forks she wanted without it being the end of the world. Zia's new boyfriend comes from South America. We were astonished because it was Mamma who introduced him to her.

He's a doctor Nonna had heard about. She'd made Mamma go to him for a consultation because she thought she walked bent over because of a problem with her spine. The doctor had begun asking Mamma if she'd had any major illnesses and had also asked her questions about her life.

She told me that hour was different from any other in all her existence and she'd felt the thrill of having someone truly interested in her, even if it was for a fee.

Zia said that Doctor Salevsky had travelled a lot and had even been to Cape Horn as a ship's doctor. So straight away we read some books and learnt that down there the dawn is red and the seals have the sweetest expression and until recently there were hunters that beat them to death for their furs. We know that Zia's boyfriend goes horse-riding, mountaineering, caving, motorbike racing and deep-sea diving and we can imagine her with her lovely curly hair blowing in the wind on the open plains, or warmly welcomed by our new relatives in Buenos Aires, as only South Americans know how.

Zia goes tango-dancing now and when she comes to see us she shows us the steps and makes everybody be the man for her, and Papà says she has no personality:

if a boyfriend plays tennis, she plays tennis, if he's a film-buff, she talks only about films. Now how's she going to go with this boyfriend who can do practically everything?

She's Mamma's younger sister and she's a truly beautiful woman, the sort that men – and even boys and women – stop in the street to look at. The best thing someone can say to me is that we look even just a little alike – I think in the sense that I'm a bit chubby and she's curvy. She has an uncontainable bosom that's on show whether it's summer or winter because she's always untidy and her neckline falls open. She has long legs and a narrow little waist, she's a metre seventy-five tall and her hair is a soft, jet-black cloud that I used to play with for hours when I was little and she'd never complain. So, if we'd been made by a sculptor, it would be like I'd been left halfway through, whereas she'd been given all the finishing touches. And if we were the protagonists of 'The Ugly Duckling', of course I'd be the duckling and Zia would be one of those good and beautiful swans that fly over the henhouse; but we're made of the same material, and I'm proud of that.

Zia has always let my brother and me do what we like with her and has always given us what we wanted, but she particularly has a soft spot for me. When I was little she would take me with her to her boyfriends' places and proudly show me off.

I'd say to her, 'Why don't you get married and have children too?'

Her: 'God willing.'

And me: 'But God *is* willing!'

Even though she's irresistible, Zia has never had a husband, nor children. Sometimes I think she was born to be a mother to everyone and a wife to everyone, which is why she's never had anything truly of her own. Nothing beats her fritters, or her *pizzetta*, or the homework she whips up for you in two seconds flat when you're desperate, or the way she explains all these historical issues to you that in all your life you'd never been able to understand. Zia says that with her, boyfriends have sex, laugh, have important discussions, and then leave. And I wonder what's missing from love, if you have sex, laugh and talk. Papà says that she doesn't have a husband or kids because, unlike what I thought when I was little, God isn't willing! And God operates with crushing logic.

2

Doctor Salevsky

I reckon though that it'll work out with the South American doctor. He's started coming to our house and Zia says it's very important for a man to become fond of his girlfriend's family. He likes Mamma's food, flowers, stories and paintings. He wanted to buy one of them but Papà told him that unfortunately he'd already sold them all. But no one thinks that he might like Mamma, so awkwardly wrapped up in all those layers. Not him who, as Zia puts it, has swarms of women buzzing around him and keeps condoms all over the place, in the car, in the dining room, in the bathroom, as well as, obviously, in the bedroom.

Papà says that Mamma and the Argentinian doctor have founded a kind of Mutual Aid Society. He's been far away from his family for years and though he talks to them every day – 'Mamina! Papino!', Papà imitates him answering his mobile phone – it's clear that he misses them terribly.

Mamma, of course, is trying to recreate his missing

family around him.

The doctor, when he sits down to talk to her, doesn't notice the passing of time and then later on he might phone her up and I guess he must say funny things because sometimes she laughs and laughs, pulling out her handkerchief, and then she asks him if he's ever tasted Sardinian *fregola* cooked this way or that other way, or the fennel and cheese soup Nonna makes, and what with the laughter and the recipes, they stay on the phone forever, because then the doctor explains to Mamma how you make broth from sweet potato, corn and veal. But then, when he finally comes over to taste these dishes, the two of them never eat anything, because otherwise they'd have less time for talking. Their meals are left untouched, they'd be the joy of any restaurant, if they ever went to one together.

They've only ever walked a short way together. Mamma had to pop out so she asked him if he had a problem heading out with her. He almost started shouting and said, 'Why would I have a problem with that?' He'd understood that the real question was, 'Are you embarrassed by me?'

Mamma got back all excited, because the doctor had got her to accompany him to via Manno to buy clothes and had asked her advice and then they'd gone into the Sant'Antonio church where the doctor had knelt down and prayed, but then he'd confided to

Mamma that he wasn't at all sure that God exists, in fact, he was leaning more towards a no than a yes. And then, in the little piazza at San Sepolcro, beyond the portico of Sant'Antonio, he'd seen all the graffiti on the walls and after making the sign of the cross because he was in front of a sacred place, he'd said that he'd cover that graffiti with the blood of whoever had done it and make them pick up all the litter off the ground with their mouths and then clean it with their tongues. Mamma reckoned the doctor was just saying that and really he wouldn't hurt a fly and Papà got annoyed and kept saying, 'Oh, the wise, perceptive lynx has spoken. The eagle, who sees everything and misses nothing, has spoken. If it weren't for your mother, how would you protect yourselves?'

My brother wants to know how come everyone in this house, except for him, has this obsession with talking about their own shit. Why didn't Mamma just keep her walk to herself?

Zia's boyfriend seems to love eating if Mamma's not around, but he's not fat. In fact he's very handsome: very tough and very dark. Four generations back his father's great-grandfather migrated from Russia to Argentina and married an *indio* girl, that's why he has such a strange name for a South American: Salevsky. Doctor Salevsky. Mamma says it's like he has two kinds of physiognomy: that of a savage, and that of a soldier at the court of the Tsar. She says that his eyes are the colour of the Atlantic and Pacific oceans when they do battle at Cape Horn and even though she's seen none of all that, it's her favourite blue when she's painting. Mamma says the reason he's not fat is that his hunger for food is only homesickness, and it's a homesickness that not even all the women he's lived with have been able to take away.

When Doctor Salevsky arrives for lunch, or for dinner, he clearly doesn't want to let her down in Society so, knowing how much Mamma loves growing flowers, he brings her dozens of plants from the nursery, in the same colours as the tubes of paint she'd enthusiastically showed him.

They're not doing anything wrong and none of us thinks they might like each other, or rather that he might like Mamma, so skinny and scared, with her floral dresses hanging off her in summer and her deportee's overcoat in winter.

Mamma must have told the doctor that she's never travelled. It's true that Papà's always off somewhere, but never with her. Papà loves travelling alone like a missionary, even though he's married, and Mamma understands this.

One day Zia's boyfriend arrived with a heavy package tied with a bow as red as Mamma's face when she saw it. No one ever gives her anything because she says gifts embarrass her and she doesn't enjoy them. Inside the package was this: *Earth from Above: 365 Days*, by the photographer Bertrand. With that book, Mamma can visit a different place each day. She was careful not to put it on the bookshelf, where anyone could get at it. If I ask to travel with her for a bit she goes and gets it from a secret place in her bedroom and she strokes its pages with the same love Rosso Malpelo felt, in Verga's story, when he stroked the trousers that had belonged to his dead father, the only person who had ever loved him. Her gestures, as we turn the pages, remind me of when she used to read fairy tales to my brother and me.

Today my favourite fairy tale is a little island in the Sulu Archipelago, nameless, because it would be impossible to give names to all 7,100 islands that make up the Philippines. It's isolated in an immensity of blue and a long way away from all the other islands, which are in turn a long way away from our world. And the photograph's been taken from up high, so high that it can only be an angelic perspective. Before travelling to other places, Mamma and I always pass by the Sulu Archipelago and caress our idea of happiness.

3

Mauro De Cortes

Ever since she was a girl Zia fancied the brother of one of her friends: Mauro De Cortes. But he was already engaged to a girl that he later married. To console her Mamma would say, 'How could he be interested in you when he already has a girlfriend?' Then Mauro got married, had some children, got separated, was sad, went out with Zia a few times and I know they even made love. Mamma would say to her, 'He'd commit to something serious with you except that he's so sad!'

But then Mauro got re-engaged, remarried, had more children and got separated again but he still never really seriously considered Zia.

History tells us that we Sardinians are no sailors, that we withdrew inland for fear of the Saracens when actually we could have built a fleet and confronted them instead of escaping into the mountains.

Just look at my mother. Even though my grandfather was a true man of the sea, she'll only go in as far as she can while still touching the bottom and she flaps around pathetically without getting anywhere. Papà refuses to come to the beach with us. Not even when we were little, when all other fathers do.

He says, 'You get too carried away with this business about the Sardinian sea. It's because you haven't been anywhere else in the world. I'll tell you how you go to the beach!'

'And how's that then?' He teases us because we go to Poetto beach with the full complement of towels and cream or when it's crowded. And quoting the Bible he sermonises that he won't go to Sodom and Gomorrah, with all that human flesh on display in the bars. Then when he's sure we're not around, when there's absolutely nobody around, for instance if the mistral's blowing at 180 an hour, or it's raining, or it's a Monday, then we'll see him returning with his shoes full of sand and his clothes dripping seawater.

'Were you at the beach?'

'Of course!' And he looks you up and down with snobbish detachment.

Mamma says, 'Maybe he's right. Maybe today was better than any other day!'

But nobody will ever know, because nobody was there.

I don't go to the beach with him either, but if we decide it's summer I wait for him stretched out on the bed in my swimsuit, and it doesn't matter that the role of the sun is played by the heater and the sea is outside the window.

'You have to be the contemplative type,' he tells me. 'One of those that just look at the sea and that's all, and if the water's not warm they won't go in.'

Then I think about how my grandfather, when he was a prisoner, had to go under icy showers, in winter, in Germany, and I say if he could endure it, I can endure it too. So in my swimsuit I run along the corridor in bare feet, jump under the cold water and call out to him, so he can see how tough and strong I am.

Mauro De Cortes on the other hand is one of those people that are really serious about the sea. He has a sailing boat he shares with his girlfriend, moored at the little port of Su Siccu. One day I ran into them when I was on my way to see Nonna, who lives nearby, and I said I'd like to watch them set sail. All the sea-going types were greeting each other and adding some comment about the wind, or about a problem with the boats, and even though they were all right there, it seemed to me like they were already far off, away into infinity. Mauro's girlfriend jumped across that 'dread, immense abyss', so similar to death, that separates the pier from a boat's gangplank, she removed the fenders, released the mooring ropes, and stood smiling and serene at the helm, while Mauro said goodbye and said I should try it too some time. Then they sailed further and further away and disappeared. Zia decided to do a sailing course herself, just in case she ever started going out with De Cortes. But the poor thing throws her guts up whenever she's anywhere near the sea.

4

Him

Sometimes we do it in the car. One of those American liberation army jeeps.

'It's like flying low in a helicopter,' he says, 'but you can look around you, over the roofs of the other cars, at the level of the lamp posts. No one can see you. They don't think to look up at you, even though you're flying low, only a little bit above them.'

Then he gives me instructions. He says if I want no man to be able to resist me, even the man I eventually fall in love with, if I want to become a swan, in other words, I have to be a whore in bed instead of immediately blurting out the story of my life, and above all I have to learn that there's all sorts of crap in the world and I have to be able to endure the greatest number of things possible. That's why he wants me to undress – slowly, like a professional – while he's driving. That's why he whips me, or gets me to kneel down and give him head and then the next day he makes a point of meeting me and not even saying hello, or he won't contact me for ages. I also have to be able to endure psychological torture.

In addition he says that I absolutely must tie back my hair and lose weight, and if at our next meeting I still have hair falling in my eyes and haven't lost at least one kilo – and he'll be able to tell from how plump my cheeks and arse are – he'll send me away without screwing me, or he'll kick me around or he'll show me what one hundred strokes of the brush really means.

But nor should I become soft, I have to learn to give him orders. When we part company he often gives me the instruments of torture we've used – a leather band, or a Japanese chopstick, or the flat hairbrush, or the whore's clothes he's brought along to get me out of my pinafore dresses. I'm happy and don't want chocolates, or rings, or stuffed toys. Nothing but this. I lose weight and I always keep my hair tidy and I hide my disguises in the bottom of my drawer, wrapping them in paper so that they retain his smell.

One day, after making love, he gave me a kiss on the forehead. He stayed like that, without taking his lips away, holding my head tightly in his hands. In silence. And we felt moved.

We'd each taken a hundred lashes without batting an eyelid and now we were crying.

Once I slipped over because if we ever go out it's always pitch black. I hurt my ankle slightly, but really it was nothing. He carried me on his shoulders for the whole of the walk up the hill, immersed in the perfumed darkness, to the sound of crickets.

I kept saying, 'It's nothing. It's nothing. You'll break your back.'

But he didn't want to know until we'd reached the car. Then he placed me delicately on the seat, as though I was made of crystal.

That was the only kiss. I've never received any kisses on the mouth, or hugs, and when I try to kiss or hug him he pulls away at once and says our affair isn't about that sort of thing. That's only for boring, slobbering types.

Whereas I'd really like kisses on the mouth, they'd give me much more satisfaction than on my feet and shoes, which he practically worships.

5

My father's God

One day I asked my father, who knows everything about the Holy Scriptures, if he reckoned the Sixth Commandment meant that you mustn't do anything unless you're married.

When he realises that you need him to listen to you, he sits at the kitchen table, lights a cigarette and stretches his legs out to the farthest chair and you see his feet poking out the other side of the table because he's very tall. Tall and lanky. With a shaved head and prickly cheeks because he neglects to shave his beard. And extraordinarily sparkling eyes, dark green like the colour of a grotto. His jumpers, always directly against his skin because he never wears shirts, give him a rough, wild air, like a barbarian, or a man of the desert.

While you say what you have to say, he smokes at you and the butts in the ashtray pile up into a mountain.

But I don't care if my eyes water. With my chin resting on the table, hugging my knees tightly, I never even change position because I'm hanging on his every word, as Nonna puts it, and when we finish these discussions I'm bent double.

That time with the Sixth Commandment, my father gave an unforgettable 'tirade' about love.

The sexual encounter means truly knowing oneself and being able to do anything, provided the other person does not become an instrument of yours. 'The sexual act,' he said, 'is a kind of apotheotic encounter. It means total acceptance. And this Commandment is extremely poetic. It tells you that sexuality opens the door to a moment of magic. What God advises against is doing it without love. It's like if he said to you, "Remember that you're an eagle, why should you peck like a hen? Why are you settling for so little?"'

And that time it was hard not to tell him at least one of my stories, not to tell him that they're terribly forbidden when recounted by a girl so young and so well behaved, but that they're stories of love, so maybe for that reason they don't displease God.

But Papà's always somewhere else anyway and it's never difficult to hide something from him.

If you need him to go to a school meeting, if Mamma invites someone over for dinner, or if there's an exhibition of her paintings – in other words, if it's necessary to show that a father, or a husband, exists – he says, 'That's not what I'm about!'

And maybe it's better if Signor Sevilla Mendoza doesn't show his face – all the women are enchanted by him and it would embarrass me to see my schoolteachers raving, like that one time in fourth year at the *ginnasio*, or that evening at one of Mamma's exhibitions, when the 'enchanted' woman hung on my father's lips until everyone else had gone home and she'd bought two paintings without so much as looking at them.

His garage, too, is always frequented by a lot of women. They're terribly attracted to this man who, as he fixes your engine, talks to you about God, about good and evil, about distant places where people are dying of hunger and the spiders are this big. And you can tell that those women would go anywhere with him.

I witnessed this only once when my Vespa had broken down, but I could tell that the scene must have been repeated very often.

Signor Sevilla Mendoza was bent over the engine. Blessed with miraculous powers, his splendid hands – like my brother's on the piano – were busily fiddling around the mysterious breakdown. A lady was hanging over him and laughing at all his jokes. Although it's practically impossible not to laugh at my father's jokes, I walked back home sadly, leaving my Vespa with him so as not to have to stay there a moment longer.

I knew full well that after a while he would ask the lady if he could light a cigarette and then he'd go and sit at the table with all his tools and his feet would poke out the other side and when the butts had formed a mountain in the ashtray the lady would think, and perhaps also make clear to him, that with this barbarian, with this man of the desert, she'd be prepared to go anywhere.

'Papà, do you like all those women?'

Then he explained to me a fascinating thing. He told me that he finds a great number of things in life erotic. A chat, for example. I mustn't think that he was doing Mamma any wrong.

'It's a bit like learning to use your left hand. What's wrong with that? I experiment.'

Besides, what more do we want from him? He works all day and this allows Mamma not to. He can take any problem and turn it into something funny for you, he makes you laugh. He knows how to tell you stories, how to convince you that God exists.

'So you don't care about those women. It's only Mamma that you truly love,' I concluded that time.

'I've already told you, I care about everything. However the woman I'd happily go to South America with has never arrived.'

6

The tango

Zia's boyfriend even gets Mamma to dance the tango. She moves all the chairs in the dining room but then she tries to get out of it. I can't do anything. I can't do anything. I'd have to change my shoes. I don't have the shoes. I've never known how to dance. I don't know how to dance. I'm fine sitting down. I'll fall over. You know I'll fall over. You dance and I'll watch. I like watching people who are good at it.

But Zia's boyfriend says it's easy and everyone can do it. He's a doctor specialising in human movement and he says that even the seriously ill can manage to walk, so of course Mamma can manage to dance. She has to rest one hand on his shoulder and put her other hand in his and let herself be carried away. Be light. She doesn't know where he'll take her. She has to have faith.

The tango begins and Mamma gives him her hand, looking at him terrified, and it's like she's been dipped in starch but this thing about even the seriously ill managing has convinced her. He smiles at her. He smiles and dances with her as though he knows about the yellow pegs and the dreams of extermination camps. As though he knows about the holidays in autumn and the squared moon. He moves her feet with his feet, her legs with his legs. The basic steps, but getting faster. Faster. Thank you. Thank you. Why are you wasting all this time on me. But Doctor Salevsky truly is a little special and in the end you give in to that desire and nostalgia for life that is the tango.

And Mamma, too, weaves her steps in and out and in and out in sets of eight and away she goes, off to Cape Horn. To America. To the end of the earth. And it doesn't matter if she stumbles or falls backwards, it doesn't matter because Zia's boyfriend makes you realise that you shouldn't think happiness is only possible for other people, it can be yours too if you try. What a *milonga*! What a waltz! When he comes over, it only takes a nod and she's up moving the chairs and running to take off her slippers. Forget about the cinders, Mamma, this is the King's hall. Forget about those clothes hanging off you. *Bolero!*

Zia says that it's better dancing in our dining room because when she goes to real bars with her boyfriend she gets the impression that all the women are involved or have been involved or intend to be involved in a relationship with him and so are watching them in a dejected, or nostalgic, or predatory way. They don't seem to know that she and he are together so bad luck, there's nothing any other woman can do about it.

Mamma tells Papà that if he at least learnt the eight basic steps they'd be able to make two couples in the dining room once in a while. Papà makes a kind of mocking gesture with the tip of his thumb on his nose and then tells her seriously that the tango is not one of his things. That he only does his things and not anyone else's.

Nonna has revealed to us that Nonno, when he was in the Navy, was the best tango dancer in the crew and being in his arms was like flying to the top of the world. But those were other tangos and there were no dejected, or nostalgic, or predatory women. There was only Nonna.

7

My mother's God

Mamma once confided to me that she's not actually entirely sure that Jesus is God. Maybe Jesus was a wonderful creature similar to God that we would all love madly. But maybe he was only a man. That's why she's always very sad at Easter. And if we ask her why she's in despair – after all Jesus is God and he rose again – she says she's not so sure about that. Maybe he just died and that's it.

She almost never goes to church. Certainly not, she says, because she thinks God doesn't exist, or she's annoyed at him, or she blames him for something. But she thinks that God's indifferent to her, in the sense that she could be at church or not be at church and for God it would be the same.

Once I asked my love if he thought God exists.

'I don't know,' he replied. 'I hope not for his sake. Otherwise he must be stupid, or worse. A God like he's shown himself to be doesn't deserve anything from us.'

'Maybe we're the ones who don't deserve anything.'

'All the worse for him, for making us out of piss and shit.'

'What about all the wonderful things and people that exist?'

'You're the one who sees them that way. I look around and I just see stinking pieces of shit.'

8

Our garden

Mamma's garden isn't exactly a garden, it's the sunny paved area that is the roof of our building. They were going to build another apartment there, but the contractor went bankrupt just after the war, and nothing was done with it. The residents of the building put television antennas up there and in the old days we'd all hang our washing out there. When no one used it for drying any more it became a space where everyone put the things they'd cleared out of their homes, things they no longer needed but didn't want to throw out. A kind of rubbish tip, except that from up there you can enjoy the view of Palazzo Boyle, the Bastione di San Remy with its palms swaying in the wind, and further up still, the Torre dell'Elefante. To the south, on the other hand, you can see the sea, the ships, and even the mountains of Capoterra, which are our last horizon.

Day after day Mamma has tried to give it dignity. The things that people had cleared out have taken on new colours and new roles. It took years and years to learn that up there, where the sirocco blows too strongly, myrtle and mastic can grow, and under the bench even violets can survive, and roses might seem fragile but actually they defy the scorching sun and the mistral, provided they have a wall at their back. Years and years of respect for the times of the day and consideration of the phases of the moon. With all Mamma's sweetness and patience that junk room up there became a paradise of delights. A dream of happiness and beauty that, for all our sakes, she protects from the violence and disorder of the world, and that makes us richer. I've noticed that the people who live in the building never fail to take their visitors up there for a look around, to amaze them, to overcome the frustration of living in such a humble place. Even down on the street people sometimes stop with their nose in the air to admire the wisteria that cascades right down to the front door of the building.

Not that Mamma's flowers never get sick or die. Many have given in to the domineering wind, or to the boiling hot temperatures, or to the seagull and pigeon poo. Mamma has a cry about it, but then she plants something else in the empty pots. And so it's been ever since we were little. The days of ivy, the days of dog-roses, those of bougainvillea: the terrace has its history.

Thin though she is, she goes up the stairs with bags of dirt and the new cuttings or seeds and she works up there for hours and hours and comes down exhausted from all the effort, but that little piece of the world is so naturally beautiful that it seems to have created itself. A gift for everybody.

Nonna has taken a dislike to that terrace, she gets angry because she reckons it's pointless Mamma working on it, on something that's not even hers. If she really worked and there were two salaries in the family we could buy a new house. You bet you can pay off a mortgage with an extra salary.

Nonna's right, but how I love going up to look at the ships framed by garlands of perfumed flowers, arriving or departing these waters to the sound of Debussy's *Clair de lune*, which my brother's preparing for his piano exam.

And how sad it is when you realise a plant is struggling but isn't going to make it, and Mamma's dejected and Zia wants to give a kick up the arse to the wisteria, or the jasmine, and to all the plants that want to die on us.

9

White women and black women

'Today you have to be really tough, you have to be a black woman. You have to put on this dress made of coarse fabric that I've brought for you. See how low-cut it is and how it shows off your tits. I like your heavy tits, they contrast with your childlike torso. You'll show me your breasts exploding out of the neckline. You'll pull up your skirt. But my hands will be tied and I won't be able to touch you. You have to be cruel: only after receiving a hundred lashes will I receive the prize of screwing you.'

For him the planet is full of shit. 'That great bastard of a . . .' 'That piece of shit . . .'

But notwithstanding his vision of a completely rotten world, he never makes me sad. He's special that way. I'm closed up in a room with the door barred and it's as if I was out in the open air. Maybe because I know that if I follow the instructions, the rules, he won't leave me. And if one day I'm able to sit down at the table and eat his excrement, then he swears to me he'll want me even when I'm old. Forever.

When I'm able to have him over to the house – because Mamma's going all around town for hours and hours in search of panoramas and then she phones me to go and get her on my Vespa – he even gives me instructions on how to cook. Something I really really like is the idea of fanning out spaghetti in the cooking pot – then you move it towards the centre and that way it doesn't stick.

Or sometimes we go to his work. We go down dark corridors with science fiction warning lights and the beeping of robots. We reach his room and lock ourselves in. Complete darkness. 'Kneel down and take it in your mouth.'

That's enough tango

That's enough tango. Since Zia's boyfriend stopped coming, all Mamma does is put his waltzes and *milongas* on over and over and cry as she does the ironing.

Zia was left with a look on her face that reminded me of when seals are beaten to death by hunters, down at Cape Horn. I can smell the blood. And the chill.

You think that if you went to Cape Horn and sat on the edge of a cliff and saw the two oceans doing battle, your life would be completely different. But actually I reckon everything's the same the world over.

Nonna's God

Nonna says that God exists, the real one. And then there's another God: my father's God.

Papà and Nonna disapprove of each other. Nonna says she could never stand people who don't take care of their own family and insist on saving the world. Zia, in these situations, defends Papà and tells Nonna that Goebbels was an affectionate father and husband but he was a Nazi criminal, and the same with lots of Mafiosi, whereas we know all about what Gandhi did, yet he abandoned his wife.

Nonna asks Mamma, 'Was your husband there?' and the answer is always no.

Then she says to Papà, 'Don't you ever ask yourself what people think? Your wife, your children, they're always on their own. People will think you're invented!'

'What people?' my father replies. 'Who are these people? Does anyone ever phone me up and say, "Hello, I'm People, how are you?"'

With Papà, not even Nonna can help smiling, and

she grumbles that he really is good at twisting people's words.

Then she goes to my brother and tells him that, if he wanted to, he could change Papà, that lots of sons have managed to turn uninterested, distant men into loving fathers. One boy, the grandson of a friend of hers, got his separated parents to make up. 'Papà, come back home!' he'd tearfully implore. So you can imagine what a lad my brother's age could do, talking to him man to man he'd have all the persuasive power to convince our father to go to meetings, to make an appearance once in a while when we have friends around, to take his family on a trip somewhere nice instead of always going alone to some poor, stinking, godforsaken place.

The upshot of this is that when Nonna says she's come to see us to talk about important matters, my brother holes up in his room to play the piano and if we knock he yells, 'Not now, this is a difficult bit!'

But when my father is around, you really know he's around. He plays lively songs on the guitar putting different words to the music, so one time he sang 'I am easy', but making up rude lyrics and someone fell off their chair laughing. The guests are entertained and they leave considering him a great friend, but then they come back next time and he's not there.

It's left to the rest of us Sevilla Mendozas to play host. But Mamma says it's just not the same and if

Papà's not around it's better not to organise anything at all. And since he's never around, the choice is always not to organise anything at all.

12

Mauro De Cortes is like the sea

There's only one man about whom I've never heard Zia use expressions like 'a kick up the arse' or 'Who does he think he is?' – Mauro De Cortes. And I've come to see that Mauro is like the sea, and like the sea he's just there, naturally and simply. Clear and calm, if it's clear and calm, and – equally simply – stormy if it's stormy. If you wish to swim, or look from a distance, or if you couldn't care less, that's your business. He accepts you, but can just as easily do without you.

He's everything we lack: naturalness and inner strength.

In the world of Mauro De Cortes, it makes sense to grow flowers or learn to make little sweets. And above all, one can hope.

Leaving aside all the boyfriends, Zia's life is sad. Sometimes she comes to see us with her defences down. She doesn't criticise anything Mamma's cooked and she says, 'I haven't eaten since the last time I found someone to eat with. I don't know how many days it's been.'

When she leaves she's a little bit happier and she says to Mamma, 'Thank you.'

But maybe Zia's new boyfriend is the right one. When we invited him over for lunch, he took her hand at the table and let everyone see that they're together, whereas Doctor Salevsky never so much as touched her in our presence. He's nice and he goes running so now Zia goes running too, early in the morning. Because, she says, regardless of what Papà thinks, the logic is that politicians go with politicians, sailors with sailors, dancers with dancers; like on Noah's Ark, you go in pairs and otherwise she wouldn't be able to pair up with anybody. None of us has come out and said it, but I'm sure the common feeling is that this time, God is willing. But Papà says it's obvious that something's not right with Zia, since she can't stay with her lovers for more than an hour or two, and after sex, some pleasant chat and some remarks about world events, she feels it's time to leave, or else they make it clear to her that she can't stay any longer.

Every day Mamma says the rosary for her and checks the position of the stars. I've learnt that Saturn is the most dangerous, if it's in opposition all you can do is pray. But I get the impression that Mamma thinks not even God can do anything about this planet, because it, too, is part of Creation and God leaves it to do its own thing.

Every day, before going out with her boyfriend, Zia phones for an update on the astrological situation and to check that Mamma is at the ready, rosary in hand, as she heads out.

A little while ago I walked a short way with Mauro De Cortes and noticed that he walks under all the ladders and doesn't worry about black cats; nor does he touch himself down there when a hearse goes by. I know he'd happily use yellow pegs to hang out his washing. At one point he talked to me about a problem he had and he wasn't sure how it'd work out and I said, 'Don't worry, I'll tell Mamma and Zia to say the rosary for you, or to check the stars.'

He looked at me, half amused, half frightened: 'Stop there, for heaven's sake! I do everything alone, including praying!'

'And what about Saturn?' I asked him. 'What'll you do if it's bad?'

'I'll shoot it down!' And he looked up into the sky, aiming an imaginary rifle.

Zia confided to me that she's slept with him even when she's been seeing other boyfriends and that it was beautiful. And the thing that struck her more than anything else was that Mauro's lovemaking was just like everything else he does: natural and strong. After lighting a cigarette he looks at you all over and you feel shivers of desire. And to get aroused he doesn't need any of that fancy lingerie; he undresses you completely without even looking at your new things. Or else he leaves all your clothes on and just lifts them up before taking you.

If I was to be born again and beforehand they gave me the chance to choose who I was to marry and have children and spend my life with, I too would definitely choose Mauro De Cortes.

It's not that he's so very handsome or charming or intelligent or anything like that, it's just that God did a better job with him than with anyone else I know and I think he must give his Creator great satisfaction. Not because he does anything amazing, since Mauro works in a boring office from eight-thirty to five, has a plate of pasta for lunch at the canteen, goes home and spends ages finding a parking spot and it's already seven in the evening. In the course of the day, I reckon he gives God satisfaction in the following way: he's told me, for instance, that in the morning he never goes straight to the office, he goes to Calamosca. He parks his car and runs along the avenue that leads to the beach. When he gets there, if it's winter it's just growing light, and if it's summer the sea is already sparkling and there's always a perfect silence. Then Mauro goes to the bar at the hotel there, has a cappuccino with some pastries straight out of the oven, listens to the news and the weather forecast on the radio, and then after that he starts work; it's boring, but he considers it useful, like any work that doesn't involve robbing, or killing, or ruining the environment. Or alternatively, if he decides to skip breakfast, he can run to the end of the coastline down towards the left, beneath the Devil's Seat. That's where the fish farm is, and he can enjoy a Ligurian panorama, because agaves flower along the ridges and the sea is clear but bottle green and with big rocks that form an underwater mountain landscape inhabited by big shoals of fish.

I've always thought of people who go running as freaks who wake up two hours early to do something completely pointless, but since I found out that Mauro does it, it doesn't seem stupid at all and I reckon that before school I might park my Vespa at the start of the avenue too.

Then on his way home from the office, Mauro stops by the little port to check his sailing boat and do whatever he needs to do so it'll be ready on Saturday and Sunday, and if there are girlfriends, kids, friends to go with, fine, if not, he'll happily go alone to Villasimius, or towards Chia, depending what the wind suggests, and he enjoys himself immensely.

So: I think Mauro's way of doing things gives God great satisfaction.

13

The world is ugly

We've convinced Mamma to go to hospital. She's not eating. She jokes that she's on a hunger strike to protest against all that is ugly in the world. For example, my brother not defending himself, or Zia's boyfriend, the jogging one, who cheated on her with a really ugly woman and Zia said, 'Who does he think he is? He deserves a kick up the arse!'

Mamma says these things with a light tone, not wanting to bring down the mood, but meanwhile, she's unable to swallow a thing. She says she can feel a stone where she used to feel hunger. Zia's ex-boyfriend, the South American doctor, was very upset when he phoned to see how we were and I told him about Mamma. He got angry, because he didn't think we should take her to hospital. We should buy horse meat and get her to drink the juice of it and go for walks, because she spends too much time sitting down looking at the view and painting.

He's right because now Mamma's day goes by like a little girl's nightmare: in the morning she lines up to wash, then she waits for them to call her up for tests, which unfortunately are very painful, some are a real torture.

When I go to the hospital I find her sitting on the perfectly made bed. She stretches out her legs, and as she talks she looks at her new shoes, which perfectly match her dress and the little suitcase containing her things. Her bedside table is the most admired by the other women in the hospital, because on theirs they have tissues, a bottle of water and the odd women's magazine, whereas she has a blue folder where she keeps her sketches of panoramas and the wooden box with her paints in it. For water she has an old-fashioned flagon made of fine glass.

When he comes to the house, I proudly show him Mamma's things, but he doesn't like them and says that they're a whole load of nonsense.

Papà once said that the only scandal is if we let God disappear from our words and our actions. There's no scandal in my story.

I'm just learning to endure. To resist even desire itself. He's made me a chastity belt out of sailor's rope. Part of the rope is tight around my waist and the other lightly strokes my pussy. When I move it's as though he's stroking me with his fingers. The instructions are that I even have to go to school like this, until he decides to screw me. Nor am I allowed to masturbate, I have to exercise patience and learn to endure uncertainty, because he might never screw me again.

My friends think it's strange that I don't have a boyfriend, now that I look better – thinner and without hair falling in my eyes – and when a group of us go out to a pizzeria and all the little couples are kissing, I admit it's difficult.

Then I lock myself in the toilet and stroke the rope that ties me and torments me. I lift up my skirt in front of the mirror and look at all the bruises I have on my bottom. And I think to myself that I have my own secret, and that consoles me.

One time I asked him, 'Do you treat me so badly because I'm crap, a piece of shit?'

'No. It's because I love you. The greatest proof of love you can give a human being is to kill them.'

14

The postcard sea

One day I discovered that Papà sells Mamma's paintings to his one-night stands and makes them donate to his Third World volunteer project of the moment. They buy them without batting an eyelid. I yelled at him, 'You make me sick!' But I didn't really think that.

'What do you want from me?' he started yelling too. 'Your mother's been able to quit work and devote herself to shades of colour. Dozens of starving people can eat thanks to the money from her paintings. And she believed she was a painter. For years I watched her ominous skies as I tried to make her laugh. Have you ever wondered whether I was enjoying myself? You always just explained it away as "Papà's a strange guy." Fucked if I'm a strange guy.'

Mamma collects postcards. Our favourites are Punta Is Molentis and the long series of the beaches of Chia. But even though they're nearby, we can't go there because we don't know the way.

We imagine the broom on the rocks, or the sea stock

with the water as a backdrop. Or those yellows and purples all velvety and mossy in the silence. We imagine what it must be like to moor at a wooden pier and walk along the path to the lighthouse, with that strip of light passing across you over and over again like a caress on your wounds.

And they're all things that God has made for us, so that we can enjoy them.

15

Nonna would have preferred Mauro De Cortes

Zia has said that she can't understand how it can be that each one of Mauro's houses is simpler and yet lovelier than the last. Because he's been married twice and had children from the first and the second wife, when he's separated he's always had to cut back a bit in order to maintain them as well as possible. He's also lived with girlfriends and he's always been the one to move out, sorting something else out for himself and leaving behind all his things, as a gift. These ever smaller houses have made him into a bigger man, and Zia says that it's not as though he has anything really amazing, but the things he has work perfectly: for instance, the winter duvets are warm, the saucepans have the right lids – those ones with a hole in them – and the food comes out perfectly. She talks about them enchanted, and Mamma rushes out straight away to copy everything, but we can't find duvets that are warm but don't cost a fortune, or saucepan lids that don't jump around when the water boils. Speaking of Mauro's house, Zia said that one time, after a discussion of the latest world events followed by sex, she fell asleep in Mauro's bed and forgot that it's best if she leaves after an hour or two, and he actually had to wake her up and drag her out of bed because he had to go out.

Nonna says that Mauro never really considers Zia, even though he definitely likes her a lot, because she's had too many love affairs and he – despite the two wives and the live-in girlfriends – is an upright man, that is, when he does something, he commits to it, whereas she has a different kind of romantic instability. But Zia says that's not the way it is, that Mauro hardly knows anything about her affairs and she's very careful not to tell him any details or do anything mad, in fact, basically she's always perfect with him.

Then Nonna says that Mauro's women were too different from Zia, who's always untidy, never goes to the hairdresser – she gets around with that cloud of unkempt hair – and dresses wildly. Zia replies that this isn't true either, because the few times Mauro's invited her somewhere, she's worn clothes so elegant we wouldn't believe it. Also, in order to conquer Mauro, she's been consulting history books for the war plans of all the great strategists – Caesar, Napoleon, Kutuzov, Eisenhower – and she tries them all. She's so tenacious, enthusiastic and passionate that each time life knocks her down she picks herself back up again. But I think Mauro would prefer simplicity and for you to be able to tell him things just as they are. That time we walked a short way together I would have liked to ask him, 'Do you believe in the power of the moon squared by the other planets? And do you reckon using yellow pegs really brings despair? Will you say "Good night" to me a hundred times with the perfect tone? Would you show me the way to the place in the postcards?'

16

For a kiss, actually two

'You have to dress in black with really fine knickers and keep me on a leash like a dog. Your uncontainable tits should be bursting out of the bodice you're wearing. Then you put me over your knee and give me a hundred blows with the Japanese chopstick, and if I complain you have to hit me harder. You ask me to undress you and I have to do it using only my mouth, like a dog. With the laboured breathing of a dog I'll wait there on all fours, suffering and whining as you stretch out on the bed naked, showing me everything. Then you'll let me get up and I'll ram it into you while you continue to hit me with the stick. I'll fuck you till I'm dying from either pain or pleasure. Until I know which of the two is stronger.'

Then one day, I was busting to pee and he ordered me to do it over him and it seemed to me a terrible thing. I was only going to follow this order on one condition: that he let me talk about my thoughts, about everything

I have inside and can never tell anybody.

'Cry away,' he says, 'There's quite a bit of stuff you have to get out. Tears and piss are similar. Good girl. Let everything that's inside you flow over me and submerge me. You'll feel better.'

And so it all goes away: the hostile moon and the yellow pegs, the loneliness in pizzeria toilets and the fact that no boy ever falls in love with me and that I don't know if God truly exists.

Then he tells me, 'Now I'll let myself unload on you. I'll piss on you and you'll lie there, stretched out, with your mouth open. And you have to drink it.'

I stretch out in the bath and with my eyes closed and my hands folded, like a dead woman in the earth, I let the rain wet me all over, like in autumn.

Little seed that I am, come springtime I'll surely be unrecognisable, with so many leaves and flowers.

17

Together again

Mamma has returned home and today she and my brother wandered about the rooms, beautiful and curved over and walking badly, as they always do when they're sad: as usual he'd been hurt at school and she could see no alternative to him either ruining those beautiful hands or suffering the beatings. I too had a stabbing pain in my heart.

He hasn't phoned me in ages.

Papà looked at the three of us and said, 'All right, tell me what's wrong. Let's have a nice collective wank.'

Mamma laughed that tinkling laugh she has when Papà pays her some attention.

'Tell me everything,' he went on. And he lit a cigarette.

But what's to tell? Obviously I don't say anything. According to Papà we're too ashamed to express ourselves. Speaking is a bit like pissing or shitting. It gets everything out. What's wrong with that? God made us with piss and shit in us too, but we're still beautiful. Sometimes I think about how much I'd like to give my father my stories to read, or maybe I could manage to give them to Mauro De Cortes, if he ever became my uncle.

When Mamma was young, Nonna always insisted that she mustn't stay out after a certain hour.

'I've waited too much in my life,' she would say. 'Waiting for Nonno for the whole of the war and then for the wedding that seemed like it would never come and then for a house of our own. I can't do any more waiting.'

So Mamma had to phone Nonna from all the houses she went to. For example: 'I'm at Martina's and we're about to go over to Gianluigi's. It'll take twenty minutes.'

And then from Gianluigi's place: 'Now Martina and I are at Gianluigi's and we're heading to Carlotta's house. It'll take fifteen minutes.'

She was obedient and when someone in a family wouldn't get off the phone – back then there were no mobile phones – the poor thing would shake with anxiety and run back home.

In spite of all her good will, there were a few times when she was late, and then Nonna would call the police, the *carabinieri* and the hospitals. One time she even called the morgue, where a nice fellow replied,

'No. Your daughter's not here. But if you leave your number, signora, I'll give you a call as soon as she comes in!'

Papà tells us these things – and others from when Mamma was young – to cheer us up. Like for instance how she had no sense of direction and when she got lost she'd call him so as not to alarm her parents.

'Where are you, gorgeous? I'll explain which way you need to go.'

'The thing is I'm not sure where I am.'

'Have a look at the name of the street, gorgeous.'

'It doesn't have one.'

'Shit, gorgeous! Describe where you are.'

Papà says that Mamma was so brilliant at descriptions that he'd immediately recognise the area she was lost in and from one public telephone to the next he'd guide her to salvation.

They were friends for a long time and here's how they ended up going out.

One day my father had to go away. He did something he'd never done: he phoned Mamma to say goodbye. At the end of this short conversation during which he said where he was going and how and why, he signed off saying, 'Bye, dear.'

Mamma replied, 'I love you.'

One time, over dinner with friends, my father said, 'Who knows why one gets married. Really, you could marry anyone. Or no one.'

'Where's Papà?'

'Where's my son-in-law?'

'Where's my brother-in-law?'

'Where's my friend?'

They ask after him and he's not around. Papà says we have the wrong idea about stability. That we think stability means staying still. Whereas being stable means being stable in motion. Like the earth – I've always thought that if it didn't turn it would disintegrate and we'd all fall off. Papà says that if they made him a nice offer on the other side of the world, he'd have no trouble turning out the light, lowering the roller doors of his garage and heading off.

Now I understand why, when Mamma would take us out as little children, on our return home she'd always smile and look like a weight had been lifted off her when there was a light on up there.

'Papà's home,' she'd say.

And I thought she was happy because Papà was home already. That is, before us three. But it was because Papà was still home.

I like how in autumn or spring the sun beats on Mamma's postcard collection. I like how it lights up the foaming waves, or the white sand, or the blue of the shiny card. My brother and I can go and talk to her whenever we like, even if she's painting. She will always stop whatever she's doing for us. My brother comes in to tell her Sardinia makes him sick and he wants to leave. I curl up on the bed and stay there. It's crazy but I feel protected by this fragile creature and by that whole load of nonsense.

'Maybe one day we can go to those places on my Vespa,' I say, pointing out the marvels on the postcards.

'Ask someone if they know the way!' she replies, getting enthusiastic already.

Once again, Mamma's not eating in order to punish herself for no longer working. And the less she eats, the more often she loses money, or things, or messes something up. And the more that happens, the more she punishes herself by not eating.

18

Will the third snow come?

Mamma says that Zia's true boyfriend will be like the snow that seemed it would never come in that poem she used to read us at Christmas when we were little. Sleet would come and just melt, whirling snow would come and turn into mud, and when everyone had eventually given up hope, all of a sudden the snow came 'shyly splendid, confidently thick'. Zia's boyfriend will come like that, all of a sudden; we will have no doubt and we will recognise him.

In the end he phoned me.

'I'm trying to put this crappy marriage back together,' he told me.

'That's the right thing to do,' I said in a firm and resolute tone. 'Happiness can't be built on other people's unhappiness.'

Not even my father's God would put up with that.

Mamma is back in hospital and when I went to see her it was a stunning day but it was wasted on me.

As always, she was waiting, nicely dressed and sitting on the perfectly made bed. So that she wouldn't see I was upset I went and looked out the window.

'How are you?' she asked.

'Good.' But I didn't turn around because I was crying.

'Why are you crying?'

I spun around and hugged her, weeping.

'That man, the one in your stories – he hasn't been in touch? Sorry for reading them, I found them one day when I wanted to tidy up your wardrobe a bit. And I know about the paintings too. One time Papà was talking so loudly on the phone . . . The thing is, you think I never notice anything.'

It was very late when I left. So, my mother had gone through my drawers, she who never wanted to know anything for fear the truth would be ugly. And it was ugly. Maybe that's why she had no longer wanted to eat. I asked my father's God, my mother's God, Nonna's God – crying the whole time – the reason why we inevitably hurt one another all the time, even those we love most.

'You just have to endure it,' I told myself. 'You have to get used to eating shit because, like in the concentration camps, there's always someone who makes it through.'

Just now when Mamma's in hospital, the residents' committee has summoned us all and said that they have obtained permission to add a storey to the building. There'll be an apartment in place of the garden and a bit of money for everybody.

Out of nine, there are seven votes in favour of the new apartment and two against – mine of course, and that of the lady downstairs. Everyone else says it's no big deal – we'll divide up the pots and planters, the canopy, the awnings, the trellises and we'll put them on our balconies and it'll be just as nice, plus we'll all get a bit of money. They're sorry for the signora, who's done so much work, but you've got to be a bit practical in life.

19

Flying

It was a period when Mamma was well and was eating. She had a cheerful air and seemed stronger.

The only thing was, she'd hang out her own clothes with wooden pegs that I couldn't attribute a meaning to and she no longer went into my brother's room to bring him juice while he was playing the piano. Sometimes she wouldn't eat with us, she'd leave a note on the kitchen table where everything was ready.

'I'm very tired, I'm going to lie down. Don't worry, I've already eaten.'

Papà, when he was around, would go into her room and make jokes under his breath. He knew if she was pretending to sleep she'd burst out laughing. But she wouldn't laugh. Not even when he'd whisper to her, 'Nyum nyum nyum nyum nyum nyum nyum nyum' or sing the rude words to 'I am easy'.

She really was sleeping.

Then one day she decided to leave, in accordance with her idea of beauty. For a while she'd been saying she didn't like the posts supporting the canopy on the terrace, that they were rusty and needed repainting.

So, I reckon, one morning she set up the whole scene. She bought the paint and the anti-rust and flew away brush in hand. It was clear to everybody that she'd got dizzy and lost her balance. But why had she put on her favourite dress? Why was her hair freshly washed and perfumed and the house all in order? Was it because she didn't want our family to look bad?

Besides, she'd always been strangely interested in covert suicide. One time she'd heard that you can die by grating a whole nutmeg into a meal and she'd said that was a nice way, that everyone would think the suicide was a glutton who liked strong flavours and had overdone it. Another nice idea, one for the autumn, was to cook yourself a poisonous mushroom after having feigned a great passion for picking them. In the summer, if you wanted to die without giving others the hassle of remorse, you could simply go off into the sea, and not come back.

I know she would never have done that job at that hour. It was an afternoon in late spring, hot and hazy, with the sun unable to shine. We saw Mamma down below, in one of the unused courtyards where no one ever goes and people leave their rubbish. She beautiful in her floral dress with her girlish blonde plait and her thin arm under her head as though she was sleeping.

I know she went without despair, or anger. I know that towards the end she'd seemed strong because she knew it would be over soon. She'd simply understood that she was one of those who wouldn't make it through and she'd fled from life just like she ran out of cinemas when the scenes were too much for her.

Papà went down there without haste and without a word. He took her in his arms and brought her up. He never said anything more. He no longer wanted to listen to us. He often sat in front of the mountain of cigarette butts, alone, practising sad pieces on the guitar with his splendid hands.

Then, one time when the light was out, it was because he'd left.

For Mamma's funeral, Doctor Salevsky sent lots of flowers, all the ones she liked best. And those were the only ones, because none of us were in a position to think or to organise anything.

The priest also allowed him to get two musicians who played a tango full of nostalgia and beauty that always made Mamma cry as she did the ironing. Then I understood that he'd decided not to see Zia any more because he'd fallen in love with Mamma and dancing the tango with her meant a tormented and impossible yearning for happiness.

Tidying the wardrobes I found, buried under Mamma's nightdresses, *Earth from Above: 365 Days*. I took off the red ribbon and noticed that something was written on the inside of the wrapping paper.

'My bright little star, I'm giving you this book because I want to share with you, who have never travelled, all the places I have seen in my life and all those I would like to see. If I didn't give you this book, I wouldn't care at all about all those places. Instead, they become happy memories because you can see them too now, and they can intrigue me because now they intrigue you too. My sweetness. My darling. My friend. My child that I never had and that I would have given, by strange coincidence, your very name. Every time you talk to me about your life I feel I'm living that same life. Every time you dance with me I feel I have your skin and no longer my own. I wish love were only a question of pheromones, because then I could have a shower and you would be gone. But you remain. I can assure you that you remain, even though you think you're not anything to anyone because you don't dance, you don't ride horses, you don't climb mountains, you can't swim and you're not a hot babe. Sorry if I'm not expressing myself well in this language, but who gives a shit? In my life I've dived way down into the depths, into the darkness of underwater caves, and I've been dazzled by the light in the mountains, I've ridden horses, I've been the doctor on ships travelling to the end of the earth, I've been with many women and some have been hot babes. But if, before I was born, the

Eternal Father had asked me to choose what I preferred and he'd shown me you, from my angelic perspective back then, looking down on you as you hung out the washing on your little terrace, all bundled up in your floral dresses (but splendid, I assure you), I would have chosen you. But no one asked me. So here I am, instead of screwing some woman or masturbating over a photo from *Playboy*, I do it thinking about how it would be if I could have you soft and naked in my bed, at least once. And at that point, just screwing you and nothing else would seem like a crime. I'd want to take you travelling, climbing mountains and diving underwater, all between my sheets.

'When you came in for a consultation, that first time, and we became friends at once, I shouldn't have let you go. Or else I shouldn't have followed you. But you were so happy to introduce your sister to a boyfriend and so proud that thanks to you, something good had happened to one of your loved ones, that I let you do as you wished. But it was your special intensity that I wanted, your eyes and your lips and your breasts in that floral dress, the low-cut one.'

And then it was signed by Doctor Salevsky.

I couldn't put the book down and in this state of emotion I went looking for the little island in the Sulu archipelago. There I found a little sheet of paper with the same handwriting.

'My child, to whom I would say "Good night" a thousand times in the tone you most desire, why do you say I use the word love carelessly? I do not use any word carelessly. I know that you love me and not carelessly, and I'm a good talker. I could surround you with words even if my Italian is not perfect. With my words I could poison your world and take you away with me. I could show you what you can't see, for example, a future that would be impossible without me. With you, the words flow like a river, easy, right, effortless. With words I could take you away, but instead I keep quiet.

'I can't risk hurting you. But my punishment is not knowing what would hurt you. Stealing you away or leaving you here?

'I will talk instead to your sister and my words will be perfectly chosen, they must achieve my goal: a river of bullshit. The poor thing, I care for her. I will have to tell her that I'm made that way, that I like all women and no woman, that travelling is my life and I can't stay put in one place, that I'm a man made to live alone.

'But with you I felt comfortable, you kept me company. You are inside me and I can take you anywhere. I have never talked to you in order to convince you of something, and I do not wish to do it now. I talked to you for the pleasure of talking to you, and so I listened to you. We found each other. I think that is love and I do not say it carelessly. It's just that I don't know what I should do. The things I've studied in my life – the adventures, the risks, the women – are not enough to clarify my ideas: that is, to tell me whether I should take you away, or not.'

A summer and a winter have passed since Mamma died. I've finally found the beach at Punta Is Molentis. A thin strip of sand broken up by rocks that look a bit like our Mamuthones characters at carnival time and a bit like Knights of the Round Table. Where the earth replaces the sand and the juniper is fragrant. A magical turquoise place. The seagulls sleep on the water, they're so tranquil it seems impossible. And the absence of wind in the inlet seems equally impossible, when just behind the promontory you've got the gale that is the mistral. I've finally arrived in Paradise and it's wasted on me, dirty and bloody as I am. He asked me to do it one more time, just once before we broke up, and in return I asked him to take me to the place in the postcard.

One day when he'd come over and no one else was home I'd shown it to him and he'd said that he knew the way, in fact he went there often, but he couldn't go with me. So now I was happy.

But something happened, I don't know, I can't remember a thing, someone was coming and I couldn't get away. Nor did I manage to follow his instructions: dive into the sea, follow him. I remember that he said to wait in that little grotto, to call him on the mobile as soon as the people had left and he'd come back straight away.

But then, I don't know why, I think of something Mauro had said when he'd come to visit us after Mamma's death. Actually, he'd come to visit the urn with her ashes, because Mamma doesn't have a grave. She was afraid to be locked away in the dark with no air, and always said that should she die, we were to put her in an urn and keep her at home with us, near a window with a view and a whole spectrum of colours.

So he'd sat down and stared at the urn in silence and I'd said to him, 'What an ugly thing life is, Mauro.' And he had replied that life is neither beautiful nor ugly, it's simply a thing that – once we've been born – we have to do. 'So let's do it!'

Mauro had understood that the thing with Mamma wasn't an accident.

And this thought that comes to me, of Mauro, of what he said, of all the times he got married and remarried and so as to maintain his children or not argue with his girlfriends he gave away the bigger house and took a smaller one, smaller each time, becoming a bigger man each time, well, with this thought something else pops into my head . . .

So I take the mobile phone out of my pocket and instead of making the call to him, I phone Mauro for help. I only say the name of the place and he arrives quickly, bringing a tin can filled with water, as well as shampoo, towels, disinfectant and one of his own shirts, because I've only been able to get the worst of it off in the sea. I'm infinitely ashamed, but soon I don't feel so bad because we talk as he helps me.

'Do you actually like having sex like this?'

'I did it because I loved him. And he loved me too.'

'I'd say he's given ample demonstration of that today, I can see for myself!'

And even at this tragic moment, I can't help laughing.

'I was happy because if I followed all his instructions it would last forever, even when I become old and withered.'

'Being tortured forever – that's a nice fate. But hang on, wasn't that Hell?'

I burst out laughing again, because when Mauro's around everything seems easy and clear and maybe even a bit funny.

'What about a beautiful love? Wouldn't you like that?'

'Sure. But it's not possible. It hasn't been possible for anyone in my family.'

'You could try looking for it. Demanding it, in fact. No more crumbs and torture. Demand a beautiful love.'

And when we return home it's night-time, I feel all fresh and perfumed and I find Mauro so nice that I even tell him about the colours of the pegs. 'Why don't you buy wooden ones?' he asks me.

'Because wood is what coffins and Mamma's urn are made out of.'

And this time it's Mauro who bursts out laughing and he apologises and says he's not one to laugh easily, but this time he just couldn't help it.

'Don't throw yourself away, little one, don't ever sell yourself off like that again, to some dick off the street who everybody knows. You're precious. We're all precious. You deserve a love where someone wants to go somewhere with you to see the place, not to torture you. Promise me you'll look for that and you won't accept anything else,' he says, waving goodbye.

And it occurs to me that in life there isn't only the possibility of being submerged in shit, or submerging others, or dying. There's also Mauro's way. And I want to run to Zia and my brother to tell them, to tell them that there's also this other way.

20

Happiness

Mauro De Cortes is the best person I know, but he stays as far away from us as the horizon at sea. Every time we invite him over he replies, 'Thank you, but I have something on.' He'd scale a mountain if we were in trouble, but he'd never come over for dinner, or to the movies, or to the beach.

I feel really sorry for Zia, even though she's a buttery doll of a woman with curls and she's bursting with health and never comes home at the end of the day without someone having courted her. I feel sorry for her because in her life there are never more than three straight hours with a man, never a night, or a day trip, much less a holiday. She knows certain things exist because she's seen them in films, or heard about them in songs, or people have told her about them.

Papà was right: when it comes to Zia, God just isn't willing.

Or else Nonna's right: Zia's the one who isn't willing. Because she's always been too exuberant, rebellious; at school they'd suspend her and call Nonna and Nonno to tell them their daughter always seemed like she was on the edge of a swimming pool and that she came to class only to entertain the other children with her antics. And maybe Nonna's right because the fact is Zia tires of everything straight away, especially her lovers.

She tells me, though, that it's not that she tires of her lovers, it's that she's afraid they'll tire of her, so she tries to give of her best. It's true that after two or three hours her lovers send her away, but it's also true that she wouldn't be able to endure any more simply out of tiredness. Except for that time with Mauro De Cortes when she fell asleep and felt like she was being rocked by the waves.

And yet Zia's not boring. When she comes over to our house we never want to let her leave, and not just now that our parents are no longer around, but even before. It's fun when she makes animal sounds, or imitates the sound of the coffee pot boiling or the washing machine on all the different cycles, or the Normandy landing on the flooded floor. Or simply when she laughs at films she thinks are funny and you wonder, 'Why does she find it so funny?' and you realise that you're laughing just because she's laughing.

When Mamma used to say that Zia was funny, Papà would reply that being funny doesn't mean making infantile jokes – and always the same ones too – or laughing at other people's. He preferred Mamma who, with great humility and intellectual honesty, didn't even try.

Zia clearly has a new suitor. He's a judge and she thinks he's Austrian, despite his Sardinian surname, because of something rigid and wintry in his physiognomy and manner, such that she's not even sure that he is court-ing her. She met him because she needed something on criminal law for her history studies and people pointed to him as the main expert on the topic.

The judge invited her to come and have a coffee one of these days, ten minutes at that bar under the Torre dell'Elefante, with the beautiful view, and as he invited her he observed her with great interest. It seemed to Zia to be a particular kind of interest, but you can't be sure.

And I wonder what man – even if he is rigid, a judge and possibly Austrian – could resist Zia's long, long legs, her short, flimsy skirts, her narrow, narrow waist, her big, bulging, buttery tits that are always prominent in her disordered movements, and through badly buttoned blouses and tops that are too thin. Plus when she talks – and she doesn't do it on purpose because it also happens when she's with us and with Nonna – Zia leans over, bounces around, and her clothes move. I reckon no man can resist a curvy, buttery doll, with her unkempt curls in her eyes and her firm, soft, white tits and highly sensitive nipples, which as kids we'd always ask to squeeze, or at least touch, fabulous delicacies of marzipan, ice cream and cream. It's obvious she's made an impression on the judge.

The ten-minute coffee one of these days, Zia told me, was not ten minutes but many more. Also the judge didn't arrive at the meeting in an elegant blue car, as she'd expected, but on his scooter, and he told her to get on, handing her the helmet he'd brought specially for her. Zia had often seen couples going around on scooters together, but she'd never got on one and she said it felt like she was on the other side of the world and it was really strange, because it's true that it was still her, but it was more like a memory of who she was. Also, on a scooter, there's no need to talk to fill the silences, because all you have to do is keep quiet so as not to distract the person driving, and enjoy the view, with one cheek resting on his shoulder. I'd often offered her a ride on my scooter, and she'd never wanted to get on, but it's pointless to try and explain it because that's a completely different story.

Then, outside the café under the Torre dell'Elefante, Zia started explaining to him what she was looking for, holding forth about certain historical events to impress him, but the judge stopped her and told her that his one hobby was reading history books when he has time and he was familiar with that issue. In other words: save your breath because there's no point.

So she relaxed, listened to what she needed to hear, laughed and made him laugh because he makes sophisticated jokes but luckily he's easily amused and he doesn't need such sophistication to be able to laugh.

Between one area of study and the next, a few secrets slipped out, like that the judge has only recently stopped smoking joints and has had countless love affairs that all went to shit and he could never work out why, since he always gave of his best.

So then Zia took a leap and revealed that she, too, had had a hundred relationships that had all gone to shit and she could never work out why either, since she always gave of her best.

Suddenly, she got up from her chair and stood next to him and proposed what Papà would call one of those impossible, infantile ceremonies: that next time they fell in love, they would give of their worst and demand the same of the other person.

She sat back down and started writing the pact on a paper napkin: Love only to those who can endure and if we can endure! They racked their brains trying to think what historical pact this might resemble, but nothing came to mind.

When the judge got her to climb back on the scooter and promised to look into the topic she was studying, it was already dark.

I imagine the snow on the Austrian mountains, a

snow that hides the beauty of what will be revealed when it thaws, a beauty I know already exists. I imagine all the animals Zia can imitate; they are asleep up there in the mountains at the moment, but they will make their cries heard when they reawaken. I imagine an enchanted castle where immobility and death reign, but where the coffee pots will begin once more to boil and the washing machines to go through their different cycles. I imagine Zia dancing the first waltz of her life and she will neither tire, nor be tired of.

21

Zia becomes a wife

Confidently thick, as Mamma's snow poem put it, love arrived, and anyone could easily have recognised it. There is no definite reason for all this. In a completely casual way, that mysterious force that makes the world go around revealed itself over a cup of coffee.

After that coffee nothing was ever the same for Zia. The other relationships hadn't changed her life. Now she went often to the judge's house, who never made her feel it was time to leave. She made pasta sauces and left them in the fridge for him, so that he wouldn't eat rubbish when he was in a hurry. She called her love by an abbreviated name, like you do with family. She phoned him whenever she felt like it without ever wondering if it would be better not to, and he did the same, and often it was just about some silly little thing that made them laugh. Zia, who had never wanted to ride with me, even bought special trousers for going on the scooter, because the judge said he felt bad if he didn't start his day on two wheels. He liked Zia's embrace in the morning, her soft tits and her cheek on his back, her long legs alongside him. If the judge didn't take Zia to work he said it was a bad start to the day. Zia told me she loved him, and I didn't want to think about what Papà would have said: 'What does it take for my sister-in-law to fall in love?'

When Zia went to the judge's house for the first time, to listen to the original version of 'American Pie' that Madonna now does a cover of, he asked her very genuinely to undress. He'd never had such a beautiful woman around the house, and it had never entered his head that it could happen to him. He'd seen women like that in the movies and in magazines, but nothing so real and above all so close. He knew he wouldn't have a stroke of luck like that a second time in his life.

Zia found the request tender and not at all vulgar, and she unbuttoned her blouse. She showed him her tits and her overwhelming body, then she sat next to him on the sofa and took his hands in hers.

'Touch me. You can do anything.'

Those were Zia's happy days. A girlfriend who was loved and in love, she smiled all the time. She was truly beautiful. Not like before: a nicely turned out mixture of meat and bone that was nothing compared to the delicacy that was Mamma. Because Mamma, walking like a beaten dog, like humanity's poorest, was beautiful to me, and I'm happy that she was for Doctor Salevsky too. Mamma had a love of life. She was indifferent to nothing. A sponge soaking up all the gifts of God. During those days, Zia and the judge were two sponges saturated with everything that is beautiful in the world. With the judge she tasted things she'd never tasted, things that are completely normal for who knows how many people, but for Zia, accustomed to crumbs, this was a feast she had only ever gazed at hungrily through the window. She related to me the splendour of a hot shower together, she had enjoyed herself so much under the water and was terribly happy. And then the judge had said to her, 'I love you,' and no one, ever, in the years and years Zia had been having sex, had ever said such a thing. Powerful. Terrible. Marvellous. 'Love me. I want to make love with every single part of your body. I want to have sex with your brain. I want to have sex with your heart.'

Zia would have liked to die of happiness and not stay to see what happened. All the men in her life had left her, why would this time be any different?

'Because maybe one time everything is different,' I said to her, without anything specific to base this on, but quite sure. And I found her so beautiful, as she looked at me, hopeful for this future that her eighteen-year-old niece said was a certainty. But it ended. Simply and suddenly. One day, as Zia was coming home from university, the judge passed on his scooter and on the back, in Zia's spot, there was another woman embracing him and resting her head against his shoulder.

So Zia went and sat on the stairs of the judge's house and waited for him for hours, staring at a spot in the air.

'Why?' she asked him, bursting into tears. 'Why?'

The judge didn't defend himself. He didn't invite her up. He sat down with her on the steps and begged her to stop crying because he, too, had a lump in his throat. He put an arm around her shoulders. That was the worst part. He'd always given of his best to all the women in his life and had felt himself vanish into nothing like a soap bubble. How many women had left him? He could no longer remember. But all of them, that's for sure. A pain he never wanted to feel again.

This time, if Zia were to leave him, he would fall on his feet. Because he loved the other woman, too, and thanks to her, Zia saw him as strong and loved him, and thanks to Zia, the other woman saw him as strong and loved him. The world belongs to the strong, as she well knew, having seen her sister die.

'Stay. I beg you. Accept me, my love. Even this worst aspect. Take me in. You promised. We drank to this.'

But Zia ran off and when she reached our place she began dashing around the house hitting her head against the walls and saying she didn't want to live any longer and she wanted, once and for all, to crack open her head and her body that were no use to anyone and that no one wanted and no one ever would. Then she threw herself onto the floor and didn't wash and wouldn't eat for days and days.

Nonna would come over to our place to see her daughter; gasping from the walk up the stairs, she seemed to get older every day. She would pull up a chair and sit down to look at Zia curled up on the floor and she would list all the good things to eat that she'd brought for her. She said yes, these were terrible times and you couldn't make sense of anything any more. The hunger she'd experienced back in her day was better than Zia's hunger now. War was better, because at least then you knew who to blame it on. First the Americans. Then the Germans. Even if the bad guys changed, at least you knew who they were at any given moment. Whereas now, who could you blame? It was obvious that the judge was a poor fool too, immature, just like Zia; after a day they'd thought they were in love, when actually they didn't even know where love begins or where it ends. Like our father, who knew all about God, love, good and evil and had abandoned his children without a penny. Like Mamma – a frightened rabbit, she, too, was without a conscience. Falling stupidly from the balcony when she knew full well how weak she was and how often she got dizzy spells. Now there were no good guys or bad guys. You didn't know what to expect, how to live. Even God seemed confused, and she would not be going to church any more, she wasn't even going to pray. War had saved her fiancé and peace was killing her daughters. Back then they'd fled into the country to survive the hunger, but there was no escape from the hunger of her daughter.

But in that prison of hers, without water or food, Zia didn't say, 'That judge deserves a kick up the arse,' nor did she ever say it after she got up off the floor. She had truly loved him and had been grateful for those days spent as a wife.

Now that nearly a year has gone by, she often says that it doesn't take much to be a wife and it's not true that she's not cut out for it: 'You get taken around on the scooter, you cook some pasta sauces, you make love and you get under a nice hot shower with your husband. A lot of people complain about marriage but I thought it was beautiful. The happiest period of my life.'

22

Zia becomes a mother

'It doesn't take much to be a mother either. A lot of women complain constantly about their children, look at Nonna. But I never have anything to complain about with you two. Being a mother is beautiful. The happiest period of my life.'

That's how it happened, Zia didn't want to get up off the floor and days had gone by and we knew very well that if something didn't happen she'd never get up again. In desperation I went to Mauro who said he reckoned Zia couldn't go on as before, she had to get a hold of herself and show some balls, and he was certain she would. He told me to relax, Zia would not die and she would no doubt manage to fall in love again and to imitate the Normandy landing if the kitchen flooded, or General Kutuzov's tactics walking backwards down the hallway. He didn't believe in God, but the force of nature was a definite reality and Zia was an equally definite part of that.

I even swallowed my pride and phoned all her ex-boyfriends whose numbers I could find.

'What's wrong with my Zia?'

Some got worried and thought I was some kind of vengeful niece. They hung up in fright. Others replied, 'She's perfect, but not for me.'

It was my brother who came up with the idea.

'I need you,' he told her. 'Don't die. Don't be selfish. I've always thought I'd have preferred you as a mother, and as a father, and as a grandmother. And I don't know what I'd give for a girlfriend as hot as you. Everything, apart from my piano.'

So Zia got up and went to have a cold shower, as she always had before the judge, and then she threw herself on the pot of meatballs Nonna had left for us all.

I got angry with my brother. 'You shouldn't have done that to our parents.'

'It's not true that I prefer Zia. But nor is it true that the dead can hear us or that people far away can have a sense of what we're thinking, or other bullshit like that. The dead are empty sacks and Mamma is ashes in an urn and if Papà could hear our thoughts he'd come back. Wouldn't he?'

The fact is Zia got up off the damn floor.

So Zia said goodbye to Nonna, brought her history books and her low-cut dresses over to our place and started her new life with no boyfriends and no money, because she wanted to maintain the two of us without having to ask Nonna for help and she wanted to buy our house, which we were renting, and give it to us, with the money she'd been saving for her marital home, plus a mortgage.

If we hadn't been so sad, we'd even have enjoyed ourselves with Zia, because when we were all together, feeling abandoned and defeated, she'd always pull out some tragic historical event and compare it to our situation.

Leaving behind the era of the Bible, my brother said, now was the time for history. We were the Carthaginians at Zama, the Persians at Marathon, Napoleon at Waterloo. We faced the battles of the Somme and Verdun, and capitulated at Caporetto. We suffered the cold of Stalingrad. We were the Jews in Nazi Germany and the Palestinian refugees driven out by the Jews. But Zia said we would pick ourselves up again, just like the Japanese.

She'd often cook something special and invite Mauro De Cortes to come and eat with us. Not wanting to be impolite, he would say, 'Thank you, but I've got something else on, maybe another day.'

Zia would wait for another day and send him funny text messages pretending to be the owner of a restaurant advising him of the menu. Mauro would reply just as nicely, but he'd still never come. When she finally decided to release her specialities, because the only real client was never going to turn up, they were no longer all that special: soft vegetables, watery sauces, dry sweets and stale bread.

And if we screwed up our noses, Zia would say, 'If they had it in Afghanistan, or Palestine, or Nicaragua, where your father's no doubt gone! If your Nonno had had it in the concentration camp, or Londoners during the bombings of September 1944!'

'Zia,' my brother finally burst out, pushing away his plate, 'we're not at war. We're just waiting for Mauro De Cortes to do us the honour of eating with us.'

We looked at him open-mouthed. How could someone who was always locked away practising, who certainly never inspired anyone to confide in him, have worked everything out? That day Zia closed the restaurant, and from then on, when there were specialities, they were for the Sevilla Mendoza family.

The most difficult moment was when Mauro De Cortes, who hadn't been answering the phone, sent us a postcard from Greece in which he said he'd taken a year's unpaid leave and bought, with his girlfriend, another sailing boat. He'd headed off and was travelling the deep dark ocean of the postcard, beyond a little white terrace with red and lilac pots of carnations and geraniums under a little Greek-blue window. Next it was a night-time terrace, the moon illuminating a yellow chair and a little table with an empty glass. He just said that he was well and hoped the same was true of us.

We got the idea that God either doesn't exist or is unjust, because we never won in any of those ill-fated battles and were always playing the role of the dead.

We didn't pray and I didn't write this or any other story. My brother decided to give up school and stay at home alone practising the piano, because he just couldn't handle his schoolmates any more. Zia decided she was through with men. Definitively. I thought regretfully of him, of those periods when all I'd had to do to be happy was follow orders and take myself off into the world of dreams. And when he phoned me to arrange to see me again and swore to me that he'd tried to carry me away that time at the beach in the postcard but it was like I was made of stone, and he'd waited hours for my phone call, it was hard not to believe it was love. But love had to be something else.

23

The vet

One of those sad days I go down to take out the rubbish and in the big dumpster next to the Capuchin Convent I hear something whining. Having learnt not to be squeamish, I stand on an old brick and look in and I see a litter of puppies of no particular breed, wet, sticky and smelly. I wonder if it's better to leave them to die. What kind of a life awaits them? One full of suffering. I'm not going to be able to find homes for five dogs and Zia wouldn't want them at our place. So I call out to the first person that comes by and that looks right, to ask him for help, or his opinion.

'Excuse me!'

'Yes, what is it?'

'There are five puppies in here. I don't know if it's better for them to live or die. I can't keep them.'

'It's better for them to live, damn it.' He comes running up. 'I'm almost a vet!'

'A vet?'

So we immediately get the puppies out of the dumpster

and place them on the guy's jacket which he's laid down on the ground.

'God is strange,' I say out loud to myself. 'He seems uninterested in anything and then suddenly he appears before you to save five puppies. I'm so happy for them. A vet.'

'And why do you think Jesus Christ's turning his back on you?' the guy asks, as he places the last puppy on the jacket.

'My mother's dead. My father's gone off. Zia was sick for a period and wouldn't get up off the floor. A friend, someone I used to be able to count on, has gone travelling around the Mediterranean in a sailing boat. The man I loved is married. Nonno was really on the ball but he died of an ulcer he'd been carrying around with him from a Nazi concentration camp. My brother's constantly playing the piano and it's as though he's not even there. Plus it's almost Christmas and there'll be just the three of us at the table and Nonna will cry and Zia will say, "They deserve a kick up the arse, the lot of them!" My brother will stick around just long enough to gulp something down.'

'And you've got no curtains left in the house!' His face lights up at his witty remark.

'Huh?'

'I mean, you're a dramatic sort. You know Eleonora Duse, in those scenes where she clings to the curtains, pulling at them, with her arms up in the air and her hair all over her face like you right now?'

I burst out laughing. What an idea.

'I'll take the puppies. At my place they're used to much worse than that. We'll exchange phone numbers and I'll keep you informed.'

I run up the stairs and knock at my brother's door, gasping for air.

'The strangest thing. I found five puppies in the dumpster and guess who was walking by? A vet. It really is true that God has his strange ways of making you see that he exists. Do you remember that bit of the Gospel that Papà used to read to us when we were losing faith, that part where the women think he's dead, "And behold, Jesus met them, saying, Greetings!" A vet, can you believe it?'

'Yes. Now close the door, please. Can't you see I'm studying?'

So I go into Zia's room.

'Zia, it's a miracle. I found five puppies in the dumpster.'

'Don't even think about bringing animals into the house. There's enough of us already.'

'I don't need to bring them home. Guess who was walking past?'

'Don't even think about it.'

The vet phones almost immediately. 'They're doing

fine. And what are you up to, puppy number six?'

I'm trying to squeeze into the welcoming folds of his voice. I find a way in. And from that opening I can see the city shining beneath my windows. It's cold but I don't feel it. It's almost dinnertime but I can happily skip it and I'm not afraid of the night, nor of the Christmas holidays with all us sad Sevilla Mendozas.

'I miss you,' he says. 'I don't know you and yet I miss you. Or maybe I should say I was missing you and then I found you. I don't want you to think I'm crazy but I love you.'

'I love you too.'

'Then let's start all over again from the beginning: in fifteen minutes' time, in front of the dumpster.'

My hair's so gross; since I haven't had him ordering me to clip it back, it looks like some hideous hat pulled down over my eyes. And I'm so fat, why did I eat all those sweets and panini? I'm such a piece of shit, why hadn't I been preparing for the chance to live? I've got so many disguises for faking love – white woman, black woman, dominatrix, victim, whore, innocent girl – but not even a halfway decent rag I can put on for true love, just shapeless bags I wear to school. Plus I'm a strange girl, too strange for anyone to really feel good around me, and I'm sad, so sad that I make people around me melancholy. And I'm afraid. I almost wouldn't go down to the dumpster if it weren't for the crazy desire to see him again, even just for an instant. So a quarter of an hour is an unbearably long time, and it's unthinkable that I wouldn't go down.

And when I see him coming I run towards him and he runs too and he puts his arms around me and holds me tight and we kiss until we take each other's breath away and then he unbuttons my woollen coat and my jacket and bends down to bite my tits and he picks me up in his arms and takes me to his car and there we start all over again.

Every so often he stops and moves away as if to get me into focus.

'My love,' he says to me. 'My sixth puppy. Let me look at you. You know you're beautiful? Your little face, your big melancholy, happy eyes under this tuft of hair, you remind me of someone, a girl I liked when I was little, I think. But I'm talking too much and I can't go all this time without kissing you.'

When I sit down to dinner, terribly late, Zia's fritters have nothing to say to me. Completely mute. And Nonna's ravioli leave me unmoved. Even the sweets in the sideboard, locked away to help me lose weight. 'At least eat a bit of fruit,' Zia says, worried. 'We've got bananas. What's happened, why won't you eat?'

'I will never eat again, because my vet is the only thing I want to gorge on,' I declare, resting my cheek on the table. And in a drunken tone, even though I haven't touched a drop: 'My raviolo, my fritter, my chocolate, my tasty banana! How was I able to live like that: without God, without love, without stories to tell?'

One day my brother appears at breakfast and puts his pile of books on the table, quickly drinks down his milky coffee, looking at his watch because the school doors close at twenty-five to nine. At lunchtime he reappears and with an air of satisfaction he says, 'Bugger my hands. Bugger the piano. Bugger everything. I beat them up and I even got them to say sorry.'

To celebrate the event, Zia starts redecorating the house, painting the tiny balcony, all that we have left now. She paints it white, and plants carnation seeds and geranium cuttings in three little red and lilac pots. She even manages to fit a yellow stool there along with a tiny Greek-blue table, where in summer she'll be able to place her glass if she wants a drink as she looks at the ships. She defends herself saying she's not a copycat, it's just that Mauro De Cortes's ideas, even in a postcard, are always the best.

My boyfriend only has a few more exams to go before he finishes his degree in Veterinary Science. He studies at Sassari and when he comes back here he doesn't like being in the city, he prefers to be around where he lives, which is the Capoterra area, which I can see from my windows on clear days. I take an hour to get out there on the Vespa, because I don't like rushing and missing out on the spectacle that is the Santa Gilla Lagoon, all pink, or purple and gold with the darker violet mountains reflected in the water and the tranquil flamingos lunching or dining. How did I become so happy? The beaches are long and they're deserted in winter. My vet lives in a house with lots of garden, lots of family and lots of animals. I don't know his family because I wait for him outside the gate, but I know the animals. They make a fuss over me, wagging tails and miaowing from the other side of the iron fence. Especially Biagio, the oldest dog, who'd be sixty-three if he was a man. He likes me. That's why my vet often brings him with us to run along the beach and he entrusts the leash to me, or rather, entrusts me to Biagio. And Biagio runs and runs as the waves break over the great rocks on the shore and spray us with salt. And I run too, to the dog's rhythm.

So there was this kind of life out there, too, and I had never known.

My boyfriend calls me by the names of different animals, depending on the situation. I'm his little bunny if I'm afraid, his lioness if I show strength. His bitch in heat when we undress impatiently and bite each other as we make love. Or his kitten, his field mouse, his little purple swamphen. But above all, no offence, I remind him of cows, melancholy and good, who let you squeeze their tits without protest when they need to be milked, to be useful to mankind. And, no offence once again, and only now during the winter, I remind of him of lambs, meek, useful and because I, too, have a woollen coat.

I confessed everything to him, including my S&M sex story. And he hugged me and told me that I had accepted that sort of thing because I used to be a delightful dung-beetle, but now I'm another animal.

I'm happy in this zoo. My vet manages to care for my wounds and pains, which are now almost completely healed. And he always has the right food for my hunger for love, for example: 'No rush, baby koala,' when I can't get going. Or: 'My whimpering chickadee,' when I'm laughing and crying at the same time. The first time we made love and we were kissing I kept saying to him, 'I can't decide, my love. I can't decide whether or not to do it.'

And he said, 'In the meantime, I'll start undressing you. You're glorious. I've never seen such a beautiful animal.'

We don't like my cunt to be called 'cunt' or his cock to be called 'cock', so we call them, respectively, 'The Island of Lakes', because I'm always wet with desire, and 'The Island of Trees', for a similar reason.

He doesn't believe in God but he wanted me to say the rosary before his exams, which he took after immersing himself in a period of deep study.

Afterwards he phoned me and said, 'I've re-emerged, you can put the rosary away, darling.'

I know he's wrong to say that, because what else could this beautiful love be but a gift from Mamma up above, or from Nonno, or from my father's God?

Nonna says that this boy's strange and I shouldn't trust him. That he's fallen in love in too much of a rush. Besides, we're too young. And yes it's true that she and Nonno were young, but then the war had come along and made sure they waited and thought things through.

On Christmas Eve Nonna's baking *papassine*, *candelaus* and *amaretti* all night long so that I can take them to my boyfriend's family who have invited me for lunch.

I stop at the door. 'And what are you going to eat? Why are you giving me all the sweets?'

'Go on, it's late,' Zia says, pushing me out the door. 'Unhappiness deserves a kick up the arse!'

All three of them look out the window and I can feel them caressing me with their gaze – I'm now slim and my hair's long and well looked after, pulled back with a hairband – until the wall alongside the road is too tall for them to be able to see me.

With my boyfriend's family you get everything in

stereo. Five puppies in great form come to the door: 'Say Merry Christmas to your sister.'

'My nonna sends you these sweets that she made, and I brought this for your sisters – *The Diary of Anne Frank*. I read it over and over when I was their age.'

'That's great, sweetheart, but Levi's *If This Is a Man* would have been perfect too. Something to keep them cheerful, at their age.'

'It's not sad, it's full of hope.'

'Of course, darling, don't worry. No one here will notice anyway. They'll throw themselves on the sweets. I'll introduce you to the other animals: my big brother, my sister-in-law, my little nieces and nephews. My little brother, my big sister, my little sisters. And the kids: Chopper, the most generous dog in the world. Shake paws with this beautiful young lady. Isotta's not here because she's depressed. The cats too, they'll come later. And you're already friends with Biagio.'

Biagio looks at me sweetly and wags his tail, and when I sit down on a small armchair that someone has pushed towards me, he puts his snout in my lap with his ears in quiet repose. He likes me. Maybe he can sense that I'm afraid of these new things, of life. Maybe he's anxious too.

'Zio! We want the story about the tyrannosaurus before we eat.'

'Leave him in peace!' we hear, in stereo.

'Let's take refuge inside his jumper, the tyrannosauruses are attacking!' The little ones stretch out his jumper and get themselves to safety. 'You'll never get us!'

'Leave him in peace!' – reprimand in stereo.

And since everyone does what they like in this paradise, I get up from my little armchair and take refuge under my boyfriend's jumper as well, sheltered from anxiety, from fear and from tyrannosauruses. The dogs and cats think the same thing as I do and bark and miaow to make space for themselves.

'You're not allowed to wear my shoes.'

'You've got lots more stuff than I do.'

'That's because I look after it well and I don't put a top on without having a shower first and I don't wear my nice shoes when it's raining.'

'Selfish, stingy, nasty viper!'

'Darling, come out from under my jumper, here are my little sisters in action. My girlfriend has brought you *The Diary of Anne Frank*.'

'I'm going to the movies later on,' says the younger brother.

'What are you going to see?' – question in stereo.

'The latest Hannibal film.'

'We don't like it' – verdict in stereo.

'You don't have to watch it.'

'That's true. You can go then. We're not giving you the money, but you can go.'

That was the first of many times I was invited over by my vet's family. Nonna would send sweets she'd made, I would take along a cheerful little book for the younger sisters and everyone would laugh at my dramatic temperament. Zia would send the elder brother, who was passionate about history, a book with some new interpretation of unresolved and widely debated issues. Then the elder brother would immediately call Zia to thank her and he'd linger on the phone even if we were all already sitting down to eat. Their parents said that he'd been an only child for ten years until my boyfriend was born, and he used to read and read and as a boy he'd always wanted toy soldiers as presents, so that he could fight wars with them, but then he grew into a pacifist who was interested in conflicts only so as to hate them more. And it was strange that in such a big family there were two only children, because another ten years separated my vet from the youngest brother, so he too, as a boy, used to read and read and had always wanted animal books as presents. Not like his little brother, who had spent all his childhood fighting with his sisters, who fought among themselves but ganged up against him.

Isotta fell in love with a dog of the same breed, a new next-door neighbour that left bones for her at the front door. She got over her depression, much to the sorrow of Chopper, who had never been able to mate with her because they were different breeds. Biagio, on the other hand, seemed only to have eyes for me.

During those lunches and dinners, he never let me out of his sight. He'd come to the gate, his tail wagging, and lead me through the garden, stopping to wait if I was too far behind. He'd be on the alert while everyone said hello, and would quietly put his head in my lap only when I sat down on what everyone now referred to as my armchair.

When it was time to go, the elder brother would say: 'Thanks, Ma, thanks, Pa. I didn't even touch the ravioli, but everyone here tells me they were excellent. The dessert too – I didn't get to see it, but I hear it was divine.'

'That's because you were on the phone talking about the Isonzo Front and then about the culpability of Marie Antoinette of France and whether they were right to guillotine her,' his wife would gently defend herself, as she muffled up the children before going outside. 'It's because you were discussing El Alamein.'

Nonna says that ours is an excessive love. That it's not realistic: always on the phone, a constant back and forth from Sassari. I never think about school, even though this is my last year. Only love, love, love. Nonna also says she reckons you can't trust someone who confuses animals with human beings. I shouldn't have told her about how my boyfriend cuddles his dogs and cats when he comes home: 'Give me your little paws because Daddy loves you. What does Daddy always say? That we'll never be parted. Never.'

I decide to let my vet read my stories. He likes them a lot. Only he doesn't understand why they always have to end badly. I often tell him that there's going to be a death and then he gets angry.

'Shit, darling, you've already killed off one, two is overdoing it. Two deaths are ridiculous in any story that's not a tragedy.'

I agree. Sure, two deaths are too much. But – my boyfriend doesn't know this – I could easily die in this story and I wouldn't feel ridiculous. I only have to think about the fact that one day he might no longer want me so much, that he might feel bored and see me only out of a sense of duty so as not to hurt his sixth puppy, and then I pray to God to kill me now, before my character has to reach the end of this story.

Suddenly I get terribly afraid that my time at the zoo of the Island of Lakes and Trees is just a holiday. And I start counting the times he calls me darling and I pay close attention to make sure nothing's remotely different from usual at the zoo. Food's never enough for me any more and once again I'm always hungry. Worried, I circle the Island, which seems less and less like an earthly paradise and more and more like Hell.

I tell myself that for some people, love is lasting: for

Nonna and Nonno, for example, for his older brother and sister-in-law, for his parents. How can they keep calm, and consider themselves worthy of such a miracle?

My heart is uncertain, discouraged, and every day I'm amazed to be the person loved. How much easier it was to be the sexual tool of someone who loved another woman, who isn't part of your story, how much simpler to live within the walls and look elsewhere in postcards.

Now that I'm out, now that there's the sun, the sea, abundant food to be enjoyed . . . Maybe if Jesus Christ suddenly appeared in the road and said to me, 'Greetings!' I'd be able to relax. He did it for the puppies, but not for me. He leaves me alone. He leaves me to ruin everything.

I convince myself that my stay here is coming to an end and I know well that having endured the whip, the Japanese stick and the shit won't be any use to me, because no one has ever got used to being expelled from Eden. So every time we have to part company, I become a pain in the neck like Mamma when she was little and I ask him for more and more caresses and good nights that will reassure me and he says, 'Good night, puppy' a hundred times and he caresses me in the doorway but he doesn't know, poor thing, that it's not enough for me. Because it's not what I really want. None of this soothes my soul. Not even the sex games I push him into with stories from my past, when I ask him to hurt me to punish my insatiable hunger for love. What I want is what he says to his dogs and cats. 'Give me your little paws. We'll never be parted. Never.'

And so I linger and I ask for more and more food, and I give him more and more food, until he gets indigestion, until he's exhausted and slaps me on the back like he'd do with his brothers.

'Relax, relax . . .' And it seems to me that he can't wait for me to leave and inside I feel only desperation.

One of these days I'll leave the Island and when the vet returns he'll no longer find the sixth puppy, or the cow, or the rabbit, or the bitch in heat, and he'll forever think of us with regret and he'll keep looking for us and he'll wonder why, why, what did he do wrong, how did he fail to make us happy. And we'll look for him too, and this zoo will be the only place we'll want to go back to. All because we're too hungry and no food can possibly be enough for us.

I'm sitting in my little armchair. Biagio is watching over me with his ears at rest. Through there is the vet with a friend of his who fell in the stream during the trip we took to Monte Arcosu. Now her clothes are all wet and he's giving her some men's things to change into. I suppose they're keeping the bedroom door shut so the heat won't escape. It couldn't be any other way. The vet didn't want us to always be on our own in that isolated world of the zoo and invited his friends to come for a walk with us. However, as bad luck would have it, the only one to turn up was this girl and of course it wasn't possible to say to her, 'Well we won't go after all.' So we went and I convinced myself that there was nothing to be afraid of, that my vet can't go around with a blind-fold over his eyes to stop him seeing other women. And everything was going fine, the sky was that still-wintry blue and the water of the river was a mirror so perfect that the woods were doubled. As we went up the mountain through the undergrowth of brambles, the river became more and more of a stream and when it became impossible to push our way through we had to cross the stream and the vet went ahead and made little bridges out of stones for us girls. I'm chubby and didn't fall, whereas the other girl – who's a ballerina and light and delicate as a feather – did. She fell in the icy February water and had to undress completely because she didn't have a single thing on that wasn't drenched. She lay down naked on a flat rock and looked like a princess from a storybook. The vet hung all her clothes from the trees to drip and they laughed and laughed together. And then my idea about the storybook must have oc-curred to him too, because he knelt down at her feet bowing like a prince. And I tried to take something off too, like my windcheater and then my thick jumper and for a while I was in my bra as well with my big tits and it wasn't all out of altruism, it was also to catch my boyfriend's attention and distract him from the ballerina. But in that enchanted frame the two of them were alone and my tits were meat from the butcher's that has no effect on anyone and can just be sliced up, and the same with my arse. When the ballerina had warmed up, ages later, and her clothes had stopped dripping, we followed the path back, and the evening gave the stream and the woods a beautiful golden shimmer. But instead of seeing in this beauty the proof that God exists, I realised that he doesn't. Because if God is God and was clever enough to create this mountain and these woods and this stream and this sky, he can't be so stupid as to let her fall in the water instead of me, or neither of us. And now they're shut up in there so as not to let the heat escape and no one from this big family is home today and in that coincidence, too, God's not proving himself to be all that clever.

So I decide that I won't be around. Biagio realises that I'm crying and pricks up his ears, lifts his head and puts his two front paws in my lap.

'Biagio,' I say through tears, 'even though I was never interested in animals, even though I'd have turned up my nose in disgust if, as a girl, they'd given me a book about dogs instead of a little love story, I was really fond of you, and all the other animals in the family. Biagio, this is the last time we'll see each other.

Farewell. Don't follow me to the gate, I beg you, don't make it any harder for me.'

Biagio didn't follow me and neither did my vet. Not to the gate, nor anywhere else.

I rush home and I'm so cold that all the blankets are still not enough for me and Zia gives me her dressing gowns and gets Mamma's out of the cupboard too as well as Nonno's bed jacket, which still inspires a bit of his strength. Nonna says she told me so: I'd thrown myself headlong into this love less than fifteen minutes after meeting him. I'd gorged myself like I did when she cooked ravioli, or meatballs, and I'd eaten quickly, in a big rush. With no class. With no logic. With no sense. And now I was vomiting from the pain. Love, too, needs time to be digested properly.

Through the window I see Death, with her badly cut, coarse black cowl. She's knocking with her twisted hands and looking at me, expressionless. I smile at her.

'Come,' I say to her. 'Eat my flesh, it's wasted on me.'

Death enters and takes my tits and my arse and squeezes and devours them and eats all the rest with that indifferent air. And what strikes me is how, behind her, the calm horizon shines brightly and the rocking of the port cradles you like when, as a child, you go on a boat trip protected by your parents. Death eats what's there to be eaten, but she doesn't want it all and she flies off into the blue night, beyond the carnations and geraniums in the red and lilac pots, beyond the ships and the cars that come and go like silent fireflies along the Scaffa bridge.

And so I phoned him, not having heard from him for months.

'You said that the greatest proof of love you can give a human being is to kill them.'

24

So is the world beautiful?

In spite of the tight black suit and very sheer stockings held up by suspenders, I spring out of the Jeep and make my way through the tall grass and the scrub and the prickly pears and the low dry stone walls. His grandmother left him an olive grove with a dilapidated villa in the middle.

He's promised to kill me one day or another with an overdose of torture, but for the moment I have to live. Inside the house he's set up the torture room, all for me. I have to go in there as soon as I arrive. He closes the funereal velvet curtains and turns on a lamp and I have to lift up my skirt and bend over holding my ankles to show him my bottom. He caresses it and compliments me on how nice it is, he pulls my knickers between my buttocks and starts hitting me with the riding crop his grandfather used to use to whip the horses when they didn't want to gallop. Until I fall to the ground.

'Do I deserve it because I can't get anyone to fall in love with me?' I ask him.

'For whatever you like. Get up off the floor and back into position.'

He takes off my knickers and goes to get the tub of water. He wets my bottom to make it hurt more. He'll lash me until I bleed and when I beg him to stop he'll just move on to another torture. He'll make me take off my suit jacket and he'll want me to stick my chest out to show off my big tits and all the rest of my meat. He'll tie my wrists to the rope that hangs from a hook in the ceiling and he'll start squeezing my breasts and biting them like he's going to devour them and this will be unbearably painful.

'You know what you have to do to make me stop.'

So I go and lie down on the tall, rickety iron bed and open my legs to show myself to him completely and I prepare myself for the torture of the strap between the thighs.

In this dark room you can have no privacy. We do everything in a bucket and then, holding me by the hair, he makes me look inside and eat. But I've understood one thing: that this doesn't hurt more than my vet and the ballerina reflected in the stream, more than Mamma lying in the rubbish down below, more than the postcards from Mauro De Cortes. More than my brother who won't say a word to anyone. Or more than my father who's not around.

25

Nonna really does have a soft spot for Mauro De Cortes

Yesterday at lunchtime there was a ring at the door and when Zia goes to open it she cries, 'My God! It's impossible! We'd given up on you!'

'Have I ruined the party?' I hear Mauro De Cortes reply, laughing.

I rush to hug him too. Big slaps on the back with my brother. We throw ourselves on him and we don't care that he went away without saying goodbye and that he didn't go out with Zia, it's just lovely that he's here.

'When did you guys reach land?'

'We didn't. I came back by plane just now. I haven't even told my children yet.'

'What happened to the boat?'

'Nothing. It's in excellent shape. It's sailing around the Mediterranean with my ex.'

'You left her the boat?'

'You know I don't like to make an issue of things like that.'

'So now no boat and no girlfriend?'

'And no house. That is, I'll have to find a smaller one, because I spent too much over the last few months.'

When he left Zia said, 'This is another Valmy miracle, kids! A small ragtag army beating an enemy alliance!'

And she started singing the Marseillaise.

After the strain of his long journey, Mauro lies down on Zia's large soft bosom, on her Mediterranean hips, on her long and perfect legs, on her eternally unkempt hair. He destroys whole drawerfuls of her lingerie as he tears it off her and when Zia has to come home to help me with my final-year History essay, he says to her, 'Stop there!'

Zia tells us about Mauro's new house, about how it's much smaller, but so much lovelier than the other one. She says that there's indirect light, that the bathroom is the epitome of organisation in a small space, that book and CD shelves are built into the walls. Food goes from the cooking area to the table through a little door that gives a wondrous quality to everything you eat. And the bedroom is like a monk's cell in a monastery by the sea, with the bed under a little window with a grating through which the light seems to come from far away, along with the sound of bells and the salt sea air.

Plus at Mauro's house you really enjoy music. Not that there's any lack of music at our house but – no offence to my brother, who's brilliant – it's one thing to hear the same exercises or the same passage for hours and hours until they're perfect, and another to lie back in an armchair and listen to whatever you like most. Zia's afraid all this will end. She's afraid of not feeling Mauro's body weigh intimately and marvellously upon her own. And this time she doesn't know which war plan to take inspiration from, because no strategy would be able to hold out against an enemy offensive taking the form of a sudden departure, another sea, another love. When she told him 'I love you' Mauro got angry and even gave her a smack on the bum, instinctively, and begged her not to use big words, because the two of them screw, laugh and talk infinitely well. That's all. And I know what bombs are preparing to fall on Zia's head. And on Nonna's, too, who seems reborn now that her daughter's with Mauro, and says, 'Finally, a normal man.'

But I haven't forgotten that for Mauro, screwing, laughing and talking represent a greatly diminished idea of love.

A refuge. That's the only possible solution: to fit out a refuge so that it's possible to endure all this.

Because it's become clear by now that none of the surviving Sevilla Mendozas can afford to nick off quietly just like that, the way Mamma and Papà did.

We have to stay. We've made one another an unspoken promise that we'll stick around.

26

Inside the shark

Unfortunately the refuge proved necessary. Very much so. You couldn't hear anything from in there, because there was a great silence after Mauro De Cortes stopped inviting Zia over and I learnt that my vet had now taken in that other puppy. This time Zia didn't lie down on the floor and she didn't run around the house hitting her head against the walls. She washed, ate and went to her university classes. She didn't make reference to any battles, nor did she compare us to the victors or the defeated. After the atomic war, we were simply wiped from the face of the earth.

The refuge, a kind of shark's belly, contained all the things the sea had brought after millennia of history; the only thing was, the life of a survivor brought no satisfaction. And above all, we couldn't understand what had caused the atomic bomb to explode.

Nonna would come to see us and keep asking, 'But what did you do to him?'

'Nothing.'

So Nonna would try to understand it, speaking aloud in long soliloquies. She said maybe Zia had behaved like a madwoman. Or maybe Mauro De Cortes didn't want to go out with a woman who'd been with so many men and Zia had then confirmed this perception by giving herself to him too quickly, without ever making him work for her. Or maybe she hadn't been sufficiently clear and he hadn't understood that she truly loved him and instead he had thought that since she played around, so could anyone. Or maybe she had been all too clear and had ended up giving him her whole life story and he'd got bored because there was nothing more for him to discover. Well, she must have done something. Because Mauro De Cortes is a good, delightful, normal person and he doesn't do things for no reason.

I thought that in the end it wasn't Mauro's fault if for him, having sex, laughing and talking weren't love. And didn't he have the right and the duty to look for it elsewhere? He surely wasn't causing all this hurt on purpose and he certainly hadn't been the one to press the button on the atomic bomb. And nor had my vet, or the ballerina. I reckon no one pushed it, not them, not us. Maybe some object had fallen on it and the bomb had exploded, or maybe it was God who had organised things badly and now there was nothing left, just the belly of this shark, all full of junk.

Nothing left. It got to the point where my brother

realised one day that his trousers were torn and full of holes, his belt had no buckle, and his watch had no batteries and always showed the same time, so he went out to see what he could find. Even the Upim store in via Manno, where he'd always shopped, was gone. He came home empty-handed and began to cry, for the first time since he was a child. He cried and said he wanted his mother and father. And maybe a mysterious God felt compassion, because a letter arrived from Papà, the first since he'd left.

27

Like Jonah and Job

He gave us his address, he told us he was in South America trying to help the poor wretches, as he'd always planned to do, except that Mamma had been such a poor wretch herself that she'd kept him here. He talked about the *cafetaleros*, the coffee growers, who had nothing. Nothing. He told us that for one reason or another he hadn't been able to free himself from his trade as a mechanic, for one reason or another he often found himself referring to the Bible and all in all there hadn't been any great changes in his life.

I wrote back to him at once: full of emotion and hope. I imagined him sitting at a table, his legs stretched out with his feet poking out the other side and an ashtray filling up with cigarette butts, as he read about the vet, about the girls that wouldn't pay any attention to my brother, about Zia who had bought us a house and had been a good mother even though no one had made her do it, and about Mauro De Cortes, about the judge, about the atomic bomb and about the refuge that seemed like the belly of a shark.

He replied at once asking me to read his letter aloud, maybe after dinner, as long as we were all together, including Nonna. He related the story of Job, who was a rich and fortunate man, but also good and upright and wise. But Satan said to God that it was easy for Job to have all those qualities because he was so fortunate. So God allowed Satan to take it all away from him. And Job couldn't understand why and he didn't know what he'd done wrong. Three friends went to visit him, Eliphaz, Bildad and Zophar, and they sincerely wanted to help him and to look for the reasons behind his unhappiness, just as Nonna did with us. But there was no truly plausible reason and these guys kept coming up with all sorts of bullshit, just like Nonna does, and Job kept on being unable to understand it all. And he continues not understanding the reason for his own unhappiness even when the Lord reveals himself to him in all of Creation, but at that point Job no longer cares because for him it's enough just to know that God exists. Then the story ends well and Job gets everything back again and dies wise and full of years.

So his advice was this: to leave the shark's belly, maybe while it was sleeping. To try and swim to the places in Mamma's postcards and see whether the atomic war had left anything alive on the earth, whether you could still see the divine wisdom of Creation with which God reveals himself to Job. And to be reborn from there, from where Mamma died.

A new Genesis. A Promised Land. Then my brother would become a great musician with a whole crowd of girls around him. But maybe with their trousers pulled up, at least until the right moment, and he shouldn't be choosing those prickteasers who never put out. Zia would get married, it didn't matter whether it was to the judge, or to Doctor Salevsky. Or to Mauro De Cortes on his return from his latest trip undertaken without saying goodbye to us, because he sure was – as Nonna always put it – a delightful man, shit he was delightful! Or to someone no one expected, after all it didn't seem to make much difference to Zia. Did it? And she'd have a son, even though she was by now getting on in years, and she would name him Isaac. And God would forgive Nonna Zophar, but only thanks to our intercession.

This ending made us all burst out laughing and Nonna said that Papà was still good at twisting people's words and she reckoned he was going to come back soon. He'd only left because he didn't feel sufficiently sorry for us, but now . . .

28

The strange and wretched Beethoven
and other greats

So out comes my brother with the same sorry-for-being-in-the-world air that Mamma always had, even though his beautiful shirt and jacket – which Doctor Salevsky lent him – fit perfectly. The doctor came over to our place to give them to him, since he didn't have anything appropriate for a concert. We thanked him profusely and he said that it was a pleasure to hear from us every so often and to know how things were going and to think how happy Mamma would have been on this day. As he stood at the front door saying goodbye he told us that his brother had been a pianist, and they'd crushed his hands because he fought the regime back in Argentina.

While he's being introduced, my brother wanders about and the space seems not to belong to him. Nonna and I hold our rosaries tightly and pray under our breath. Zia says that if it doesn't work out, my brother could become a surgeon, what with those splendid hands.

Or as the judge always says – when he comes by from time to time to pick up Zia, who holds no grudge against him and is now friends with him – he could study law, since he has a strong sense of justice. He could give music a kick up the arse.

But when my brother plays, the strange and wretched Beethoven and other greats have the better of everyone and everything. Because that music contains the fragile, tragic, joyous and divine intensity of life. All his schoolmates are there, and his female admirers and what's left of the Sevilla Mendoza family, and the applause is never-ending.

29

And now that the shark is sleeping?

Papà hadn't really been clear and he wasn't around to ask. As usual. We wondered what this new genesis really was and what it actually meant to start over from where Mamma died, what it meant to look around for the power of God to be revealed to us.

The shark was gnashing its teeth and was never going to leave an opening between one tooth and another for us to get out. I dreamt that we would escape one starry night, all four of us, and that we would swim into the calm, warm womb of the sea. We would stick together and even Nonna would make it through. We would reach the beach in Mamma's postcard and perhaps we'd start over from there. Something would spring to mind. But none of them wanted to come along.

So one hazy spring afternoon, similar to the one when Mamma had died, I took my Vespa and decided to go there on my own. I was a bit scared of the cliffs along the road to Villasimius, but the sea was so calm and beautiful and light that it blended in with the clouds.

That's how God was with us people: tranquil and serene and infinitely distant. We always had to get out of the shit by ourselves. Whereas I would have liked some instructions. Papà said that to escape from the shark's belly you have to wait until it's sleeping, but how can you tell if it's sleeping? And how can you tell what the real shit is?

Then it occurred to me that nothing in my life was or ever had been shit. Damn it, actually, everything was beautiful. In Mamma's life too, except that she had never understood that. And neither had Zia. Or Nonna. Nor even my brother, or my father.

It had been a beautiful holiday at the zoo with the vet and it certainly hadn't been a mistake to sit at his table and gorge myself with no class, since I was so hungry. It had been beautiful to let myself be carried off into another world by him and to get to hear the bad guys' side of things. It had been beautiful for Zia to play the wife and mother and to learn to swim and to grow geraniums and carnations on the balcony. It was beautiful for my brother to have Beethoven and the other greats and all those girls that hadn't arrived yet but would come. It had been beautiful for Mamma to have those tangos and for Papà to have Mamma and for her to have him and for Nonna to have us all. It's just that we didn't understand it. Everything was beautiful because I loved them. I wouldn't want to meet anyone but them in my life. And I finally realised that God's not stupid at all and he knows perfectly well what he's doing. And nor is it true that there's no way of getting to beautiful places and that we're unable to enjoy them. Instead of taking the road with the cliffs I went the other way, towards Chia, where there are long dunes of soft sand. I parked the Vespa next to a hut and walked along one of the perfumed paths. Myrtle. Juniper. Rosemary. Even the poor thistle flowers showed off the colour of the lilac, as they found an opening under the stones.

So, an insignificant dot in the universe, I prepared to enjoy that gift from God in the true sense of the word. When I reached the dunes I sat down, took off my shoes, and looked at the descent of white sand that, like a slide, would carry me sweetly into the water, the blue, clear, infinite water. Not only was God not stupid, he was brilliant.

And I realised that was the moment to escape, because I was happy not about what was happening, but about the simple fact that I existed, and I could tell that this was the right idea and that the shark was now sleeping. That was when I saw an opening between its teeth, I slipped through and let myself slide down on the sand and be carried away by the delicate current of the sea and I knew that I would make it and that I would become wise and full of years like Job.

The world truly is beautiful

With his instructions, the strap and a bit of manure I've turned from the ugly duckling I was into a swan. There's no more talk of killing myself, even living like this is beautiful. When we cross the threshold of the house, all creaking and rickety, he takes me in his arms and carries me up the stairs. I manage to cook spaghetti with it fanned out nicely in the pot so that it doesn't stick, and I wander through the rooms of my palace, and he bathes me in the tub after the torture, and I bring him coffee holding the saucer in my mouth and walking on all fours, wearing a corset and a chain around my ankle. We never talk because getting to know each other and sharing our stories is not part of the game. If I want to talk I go to Papà's garage and between one engine and the next he's always ready to sit down and listen to me and smoke his cigarettes at me. I love the walk to his garage, I love his feet poking out the other side of the table, I love the fact that he now works twice as much as before because he brought María Asunción back from South America, for his son I think, since she spends all her time in adoration of my brother at the piano.

And we all find her delightful and think that the boy truly has found America. Nonna screws up her nose and says she's too dark though, too *indio*, not like those glorious South American women you see on TV, and she says that we're all into strange things and now all of a sudden 'you can't even take a piss or a shit' without María Asunción. But she cooks ravioli and meatballs for the girl and whenever she wants anything Nonna's at her command.

Zia's packing her suitcase because Doctor Salevsky has invited her to Argentina, as a friend. They'll go to Cape Horn and to Iguazu Falls and all his relatives will be there at the airport to welcome them, affectionate as only South Americans can be.

The only thing is I reckon Zia's fallen in love with Papà, but they're light years apart. I'll never forget the time my father went to look for something in her room – which used to be Mamma's little studio – and found a whole pile of books on the desk. And I don't know why, but instead of pretending it was nothing, he took them and then he came to dinner dressed up as an exorcist, threw them on the table and started reading out their titles in a solemn tone:

'*How to Conquer a Man Through his Stomach*;

It's Easy to Become a Queen of Sex; *How to Handle Arguments with the Man You Love*; *How to Be a Second Wife*; *You Can Be a Geisha Without Ever Setting Foot in Japan*; *What All Men Find Irresistible in a Woman . . .*'

Then he grabbed Zia by her mass of curls and holding her tight like that he made her read out the titles with him.

'You read them too, creature possessed by the devil! These are your sacred texts, your Bible which offends the complexity of Creation!'

We laughed until we cried and Zia was angry but you could tell that from time to time she couldn't help laughing herself. In the end she took all Satan's works, put them in a rubbish bag and went downstairs to throw them in the dumpster.

And it's clear that Zia now prefers our kitchen to Cape Horn, sailing boats and all the rest, but that's life.

31

The storm

Then one day we overdo it. He wants me to feel ridiculous, he says we're all ridiculous. That's why I have to go around naked with a scrubbing brush attached from behind and I have to clean the floor like that, but with each tile the handle goes further in, causing excruciating pain.

I start to feel sharp pains in my stomach. Terrible nausea. A pool of blood forms on the floor. I want to go to my real home, to my family, but how can I in this state. That's why I give him Mauro De Cortes's mobile number and address. I feel sure he's returned. It's a scientific fact that he's always there for me.

'You can just drop me outside the front door of the building and leave.'

'Fuck that. I'm taking you to hospital.'

He picks me up in his arms and like that other time he places me delicately on the seat of the car as though I was made of crystal. He tears off with a squeal of the tyres leaving behind our world with the door open, the bed unmade and all the traces of his secret love.

'You can just drop me at the front door,' I keep begging. 'Why do you want to get yourself into trouble?'

'Be quiet. Even on the point of death you can't shut up.'

I don't remember a whole lot more, apart from him cursing the stupidity of God, and yelling at the piece-of-shit doctors in the Emergency Room for not throwing everyone else out to make space for me, and also taking one doctor by the scruff of the neck and threatening to kill him so the doctor calls the police and he has to give his particulars and all that.

Then nothing. I'm stretched out in a clean, perfumed hospital bed and Mauro's there holding my hand tightly and stroking my head without tiring and fixing my hair constantly as if I were about to go to a party.

'So, the Sardo-Masochist has struck again. Don't laugh, you silly little girl, it's bad for you.'

'Did you see each other?'

'Who? I didn't see anyone. A dickhead criminal phoned me and told me where to come to collect you.'

'So that was you yelling.'

'Afterwards I apologised. We have to inform your family, little one. The official version is peritonitis.'

32

María Asunción

Here in hospital there's plenty of time for everything. It would be nice to write a little about María Asunción.

For the first time in his life my brother asked my father for something: to extend the girl's summer stay. Actually, her time was up already, because the association Papà belongs to had only managed to get one month. It's gone quickly.

María Asunción is twelve, maybe thirteen. My father met her at the market where she lived with other kids, eating when she could, sleeping in fruit crates and selling whatever she could find in the rubbish. He didn't follow her – she was the one that followed him, timid and shy as she is. When Papà wandered around the market with the other volunteers, he'd always come across her along the way. So he'd ask her about her life and she'd say playful things, I'm sure she was irresistible. But it's not like my father got too familiar with her, at the start he thought she was trying to make a bit of money by offering herself to him, as the girls down there often do. But no. María Asunción would put her hand in Papà's and want to walk a little way with him, joking around. One day my father discovered that María Asunción is an artist, because she turned up with a jar full of little stones and sand with which she made a marvellous sound, as she sang like a siren. That day my father simply couldn't joke around and he burst into tears and told her how his son is a pianist and plays all day long and thinks of nothing but music and how much he'd like her to meet him.

So they went looking for María Asunción's mother, who lived with her second husband, from whom the child had fled after an attempted rape. A failed attempt – she was lucky and had only ever made love with kids like herself and never with adults, plus she had her music and her singing.

Nonna immediately wanted her to live with her and sleep on the soft mattresses of her daughters' beds and taste her most delicious foods.

I think María Asunción is the reincarnated daughter of Atahualpa: utterly regal. She won't touch so much as a trinket in Mamma and Zia's room without being invited to do so over and over and she won't eat until she's sure everyone's had their fair share and we've convinced her that if she doesn't eat those things, we'll be throwing them out. Then her face lights up.

'*Muchas gracias*!' says our *indio* princess with her

long straight hair, fine fingers and skinny legs.

When she comes over to our place she spends her time in adoration of my brother playing the piano and my father has convinced her to make one of her musical instruments. So one day, early in the morning, we went to Poetto beach so that she could find little stones and sand to put into jars and the sea was as calm as in a bathtub. Not too much wind. Not too hot. Not too many people. She was afraid, so to show her there was nothing to be scared of we all dived in, even Nonna. And all you could hear was our breathing with every two or three light strokes and the sound of the last wave on the shore. My brother turned around and convinced María Asunción to climb on his back and she trusted him and joined with ours her breath, her light strokes, and her princess's feet among the shoals of silvery fish. I was sure she was finding the opening between the teeth of her own shark now that it was sleeping, and that my father would contrive a way to keep her here with us.

Getting to know María Asunción I'm more and more convinced that the whole world suffers the same hunger. Every night, before we go to bed, we have to phone and reassure the little girl that we're alive.

'*Buenas noches,* María Asunción!'

'*Buenas noches*!'

'*Buenas noches*!'

Nonna says only after that will María Asunción go

to sleep. And in the morning it's the same ceremony again to let her know that we've woken up safe and sound.

'*Buenos días,* María Asunción!'

'*Buenos días!*'

'*Buenos días!*'

Then one day my brother comes back from the conservatorium and happily informs us that he's won a scholarship and he'll be going to Paris to finish his studies.

Who's going to tell María Asunción tonight?

33

Who will put the shark to sleep?

Nonna says she doesn't need much to be happy: if Mamma and Nonno hadn't died, if Papà hadn't left, if Zia got a boyfriend, if my brother phoned from Paris more often and told us about things, if I were cured . . . If God were willing.

Mauro De Cortes has ended it with the latest girlfriend. He often runs into Zia here at the hospital. One day she was carrying some heavy bags with everything I needed and he ran up to take them from her. After he'd left, Zia couldn't stop repeating, 'Did you see how he took the bags?'

When my father arrived, she just couldn't stop herself telling him too and Papà replied, 'And you said he wasn't in love with you. Fuck that! This business with the bags is clear evidence.'

Zia went quiet and you could tell she felt silly, but I could also tell that Papà is jealous.

And yet Mauro De Cortes isn't a bad person. Or an unfaithful cheat who deserves a kick up the arse, as

Zia puts it. Of course nor is he as delightful as Nonna maintains. But I consider it a privilege to have known him.

When he comes to visit me he tells me about the sea and about sailing. I think Mauro didn't want Zia because she doesn't know how to sail and sailing means that you have to study the situation carefully: wind, currents, distances, depths, lighthouses. And then you have to act accordingly. Mauro says that for a sailor to have a bit of fun you need at least five knots and at five knots Zia's vomiting is something special. I know because she and Mamma used to stuff themselves with Dramamine even just to get the ferry from Calasetta to Carloforte and Nonno would say, 'And you're supposed to be the daughters of a sailor?'

But then why did Mauro dump all those ladies who didn't vomit? One time I asked him and he replied that I really am a character. Who said it was him that dumped them?

They dumped him, you bet. Sick of his silences, the long interminable days without seeing anything but sea, his inability to give compliments, his obsessions. But for him, the pleasure of the sea remained unsullied. The concreteness of the actions you take. You study the winds and put up the right sail. You catch fish and eat them.

Because the joy of sailing is sailing!

If it hadn't been for Mauro and the hospital, I wouldn't have learnt all sorts of things about Mamma, about when she was a girl. He's known Mamma and Zia forever because he lived in the building opposite, in the Basilica di Bonaria neighbourhood. Mamma never went to parties except when she was dragged along by friends or else practically forced by Nonna. She'd sit there frightened as a rabbit, and if anyone asked her she'd say she didn't know how to dance. She'd hide in the bathroom for almost the whole party. She had beautiful straight blonde hair tied back in a plait and eyes as sweet as chocolate but she never hit it off with boys. Even walking a short way with her was a huge undertaking because you could tell she felt anxious and didn't know what to say. The atmosphere got heavier and heavier and it became more and more embarrassing. As a boy he thought she must be a bit sick. I mustn't be offended – it was because of the way she walked, all curved over, zigzagging, inside those floral bags and those shabby old-fashioned shoes.

My father always invited her everywhere and she'd wait until he'd finished dancing with the other girls. Then he'd go up to her so they could go home together and he'd take her plait and shake it like a tail, saying, 'Woof! Woof! Arf!' Any other girl would have called him a dickhead but not her. She'd laugh like she never laughed with anybody else. Because Papà was her exact opposite: swarms of girls after him. He was a guitarist, a brilliant self-taught musician, he had it all. He'd do anything to get people to laugh, even getting himself into trouble. He talked to the stones and the stones talked to him. He wanted to save the world – as a revolutionary, as a priest, who knew – and it was as though he was starting with that strange creature that was my mother. And in the end he succeeded, because for almost a quarter of a century he was able to save her from the storm.

But when the storm arrives it can be unexpected. Mauro knows because he's experienced it.

To begin with you enjoy the wind, because it's precisely what a sailor wants. But then it blows harder and harder. Sixty, seventy knots. You reef the sail. Every movement becomes difficult, risky. You have to tie yourself down, but once he didn't manage to do it in time. It was too late and he couldn't let go of the rudder even for a moment. Seven hours at the rudder in the driving rain. So violent it ripped out a table bolted down at the bow. He had no point of reference in a world of watery fury. He might lose the sail, the mast might snap. The only thing to do was to keep the boat going at least a little bit and endure it. At that point Mauro had understood that he might die, he resigned himself to it and began to admire the scenery, even though he was frozen and numb. He enjoyed the height of the waves and that space without land, or sky, just water vaporised by the wind. And then it passed. Mauro had made it.

The story of the storm frightened me so much that the other day, when it started raining, I sent my father a text message: 'I forbid you to come to the hospital, there's a storm.'

Straight afterwards my mobile rang. 'What storm, my girl, a storm in a *teacup*?'

34

The new Sevilla Mendoza family

Standing up outside the church. Dark glasses to cover the tears that are falling in big drops. The people coming out of the previous mass look sympathetic and then keep on going. Someone comes up.

'Is there a funeral next?'

'No,' Nonna bursts into sobs. 'Nobody's died. We're crying with happiness. Today my daughter is marrying my son-in-law. It's the only way for María Asunción to stay with us, God willing.'

And God is willing! I say.